DENNIS

AND THE

Studio Press
An imprint of Kings Road Publishing
Part of Bonnier Publishing
The Plaza, 535 King's Road,
London, SW10 0SZ

www.studiopressbooks.co.uk

www.beano.com

Written and illustrated by Nigel Auchterlounie

A CIP catalogue record for this book
is available from the British Library.

Paperback: 978-1-78741-278-1

Printed and bound by Clays Ltd, St Ives Plc

2 4 6 8 10 9 7 5 3

MIX
Paper from
responsible sources
FSC® C018072

Studio Press is an imprint of Bonnier Publishing company
www.bonnierpublishing.co.uk

AN EPIC BEANO® ADVENTURE
DENNIS
AND THE

STUDIO
PRESS

A WORD FROM THE AUTHOR

"Stop kicking that ball against my wall! I'm trying to write a book in here!"

That was the first thing I ever said to Dennis, shortly after moving to Beanotown. Other things I've said to Dennis have been:

"That dastardly dog of yours has dug a hole in my lawn!"

"Build a tent in your own garden!"

"Which idiot bought you a trumpet?!"

We're not even neighbours. He lives three doors down from me.

I moved from London to get far away from the hustle and bustle of the capital, as I need quiet for my writing. I chose Beanotown because the house prices here are incredibly cheap and, being an author, I can work anywhere. At the time, I didn't know why house prices are so cheap here. It took me a week to figure out that the place is plagued by strange, unbelievable coincidences and very naughty children. In fact, it's hardly ever quiet.

But how did I come to write this book?

Well... I was on the phone to my publisher and she was not happy. My last book, *Eleven Everyday Uses for Moss*, hadn't been a huge success and my publisher was hoping that my next book would sell more than eight copies.

"**Nobody** wants to read about moss or mould or damp or any of that!" she shouted down the phone. "Just write a funny story about a... er..." She paused for thought. "An exciting story with action, magic, baddies and a disaster to avoid, or something."

I thought long and hard about this. *How could I possibly come up with a crazy story like that?*

Then it hit me.

A football, straight in the face!

It had come through the window and flattened my nose.

5

"Hey! Writer dude!" came a familiar voice. "Can I have my ball back?"

"That's the **ninth time** this ball has hit me in the face!" I shouted back, leaning out of the window.

"Keep the ball if you want," said Dennis. "But I should to warn you, my dad's a cage fighter!"

"I know your dad," I cried. "He works at the paper-clip factory!"

"Yeah, as a cage fighter!" Dennis answered.

"Paper-clip factories don't need cage fighters," I pointed out. "Can't you keep out of trouble for at least one day?!"

"I doubt it," replied Dennis, laughing.

Then it hit me.

No, not the football again. I still had that.

An idea!

"If you want your ball back, you'll have to tell me a story. Tell me about some of your adventures."

"I don't have 'adventures'! Just gimme the ball back," Dennis protested. "Nothing ever happens in this boring town. Except maybe that time I ended up in the tunnels under Beanotown, where there were these weird steam-powered robots some Viking scientist had made. Or the time I got into an all-out war with the Headless Headmaster of Horrible Hall. Or those times with the dinosaurs on Duck Island...

Or the time Gnasher ate something else he shouldn't and grew as big as an elephant... or the time Santa got mad at me, even though it wasn't me who kidnapped him! That was Minnie. I just got dragged into that one! Or the time the town was almost destroyed by a huge tidal wave of uncontrollable nonsense, or the time..."

"**That one!**" I shouted. "Tell me about the uncontrollable nonsense thing."

So he did.

It wasn't easy. The first time Dennis recounted the tale, he said: "Well, there was like this thing in a place and stuff went wrong, so it all kicked off, but I totally sorted it. The end."

I knew for a fact that my publisher would want a little more detail than that. It took a while to get all the detail I needed and for the parts Dennis wasn't there for, I had to interview other people (including a ghost and an alien!). But now I'm sure I've managed to piece together the entire astounding story of *Dennis and the Chamber of Mischief*! And what a story it is.

I've also done the drawings, because no one thought to take any pictures at the time.

THE BIT BEFORE THE OPENING CREDITS

Eeny, meeny, miny, moe, thought the huge asteroid as it floated through space 65 million years ago. *Which planet shall I crash into?* That's always a very tricky question for an asteroid to answer.

It had gone past a tiny one, which wasn't much of a planet at all. Then a blue one. Then a nice red, rocky one in which the asteroid thought it could leave a lovely crater (asteroids love to leave craters in things). But then it spotted a cheeky blue-and-green planet and immediately disliked it. It seemed to be saying, "Aren't I awesome? I've got a breathable atmosphere! I've got life on me. Look!" Just like that kid at school who gets better birthday presents than you.

So Dennis, the asteroid, crashed into Earth.

Did I mention the asteroid was called Dennis? Well, it was. How do I know? I just named it!

Dennis crashed into the bit of Earth that would become Beanotown 65 million years later. It burnt through the atmosphere, heating up to a million degrees and bursting into some really quite satisfying flames, before smashing into the planet with enough force to rip open time itself.

The explosion threw enough dust into the atmosphere to black out the Sun for years, resulting in a ten-year-long winter, which killed all but a few of the dinosaurs.

The explosion had also ripped open a hole in time and blown a sort of giant bubble that bounced forwards, into the future. In it were caught 59 dinosaurs of various types. *Whoa!* they thought. *We're caught up in a floaty time bubble! We hope it drops us off somewhere safe.*

Eventually, the time bubble full of dinosaurs came to rest 11 years after Dennis, the asteroid, hit. Just as the sun was beginning to shine again. Their descendants still live in Beanotown now – on Duck Island, in the middle of the park.

I know what you're thinking... 65 million years is a bit far back to begin a story about a ten-year-old boy. It takes starting at the beginning to a whole new level and it may feel like this bit hasn't got anything to do with what follows, but just stick with me.

Or have a look at the end.

BORED

Dennis was bored. This is a different Dennis. This isn't Dennis, the asteroid, which caused an extinction-level event 65 million years ago. This is Dennis the ten-year-old boy with naturally spiky hair, a red-and-black striped woolly jumper and a super-low boredom threshold. You know? From that bit at the start in my garden.

That Dennis.

No relation to the enormous asteroid.

All his games were played out and YouTube had nothing on worth watching. It was a lovely sunny day. The sort of day parents say their

ten-year-old kids should be 'out and about' doing something, but Dennis wasn't in the mood. He was lying upside-down on the sofa.

"I'm **bored!**" he shouted to the living room.

"If you're bored," his mum called from the kitchen, "why don't you..."

Dennis didn't wait to hear the end of the sentence. He jammed his fingers in his ears, rolled off the sofa and ran out of the house.

To avoid Mum, who sounded like she was in the kitchen, Dennis dodged out of the front door.

The problem with this was that his skateboard was in the back garden. So he opened the garage door just enough to squeeze beneath it, then battled his way through the ceiling-high mess, to the door at the back of the garage.

Dennis always enjoyed this route. It was fun to clamber over ladders, climb through tyres or old wardrobes with no backs, then squish himself between boxes and under stinky old carpets.

Eventually, Dennis stumbled out of the garage into the garden, covered in cobwebs.

Dennis's dog, Gnasher, looked up from his spot in the sun, then went back to sleep. He'd had a tiring morning digging up various gardens around the town. Now, sleeping was required.

Dennis looked around. There was no sign of his skateboard. He was sure he'd left it here. Well, Mum had left it there, after throwing it out of the kitchen window when she walked in on him trying to

'drop in' off the sink. (If there are any loser parents reading this, 'dropping in' is when someone cooler than you starts skating/BMXing/scooting from the top of a ramp). But now the skateboard had gone!

Dennis said the only thing you can say in a situation like this: **"Urrrgh!"** Then he said, "Come on, Gnasher, let's get out of here!"

Gnasher, though, was comfy and cosy in the sun. He lifted his head and gave Dennis a look that said *I'm gnot coming. I had a busy morning digging up that writer dude's garden, and gnow I'm tired and just want to relax.*

Gnasher has very expressive eyes (and no, I didn't spell 'not' and 'now' wrong. Gnasher is so growly and gnashy that words starting with an N end up starting with a G).

"Urrrgh!" Dennis repeated.

Things weren't going well. No skateboard and now no Gnasher? Dennis seemed to have lost his usual awesomeness.

A LOSS OF AWESOMENESS

Thinking about it, Dennis's usual awesomeness had been missing for a while. The day before he'd had the amazing idea to climb a tree in the park and throw water balloons at people. There were no water balloons in the house, but he had found some old, unused balloons left over from his birthday with 'Happy 10th Birthday' on them. That seemed ages ago now (sometimes Dennis felt like he'd been ten for more than sixty years).

The small problem with throwing huge birthday balloon water balloons at people from a tree was that you had to climb the tree first... while carrying huge birthday balloon water balloons at least five times the size of normal water balloons.

Dennis stuffed them up his jumper and they burst before he got as far as the first branch. Soaked and surprised, Dennis had fallen to the ground right in front of Gnasher, who had given him an I-don't-think-you-wanted-to-do-that look.

Then there was the time either before or after that, when he'd decided that a rope swing over the stream in the woods would be awesome. He'd made it without incident, but when it came to trying it out, the stick handle had snapped and he'd fallen – SPLOTCH! – into the muddy bit between the water and the grass. The muddy bit was, pretty much, only as wide as Dennis.

A centimetre to the left or right and there would have been a tiny part of him that hadn't fallen in the mud.

Something wasn't

right. What had happened to Dennis's usual menacing luck? Where had all his awesomeness suddenly gone?

The first sign of the awesomeness loss was before all that.

Dennis was having a water battle with... well... everyone who walked past his house. These were all one-sided water battles, as the people walking past hadn't thought to bring their water blasters with them. Sergeant Slipper, Dennis's teacher Mrs Creecher, a plumber, a baker, a candlestick-maker, a

quantity surveyor, a shop assistant, a cartoonist for a popular weekly comic – everyone fell into Dennis's sights. Gnasher, too. Dennis wasn't being cruel, though. Gnasher liked getting squirted at! He liked to bite, chomp and gnash the squirt.

"Gnasher!" Dennis shouted, after Gnasher had jumped in front of, and gnashed, a squirt meant for a cable-TV engineer. "Quit getting in the way!"

Gnever! thought Gnasher. He liked this game.

Before Dennis could try again, the water blaster decided for him and started leaking in a very unimpressive way. It really wasn't the sort of thing that usually happened. In Beanotown, if a water blaster breaks, it explodes, soaking whoever is holding it. This was just a heavy trickle down Dennis's arm.

Gnasher saw that the fun was over. Standing under a drippy elbow just didn't have the same feel to it as gnashing the squirt. So Gnasher went inside.

SPLOOOOOOOOSH!!!

Dennis was suddenly completely soaked!

"Ha! Ha! Ha!" Walter laughed from far, far down the road.

Dennis and Walter were arch-enemies. It was a bit of a one-sided arch, if truth be told. While Dennis didn't particularly like Walter, Walter hated Dennis with a passion. He seemed obsessed with him and was constantly drawing up revenge plans against Dennis. Revenge for a quarrel so old neither of them could remember it.

He squirted Dennis again with his super high-powered 'assassin-grade' water blaster.

He was so far away! Walter was only the size of your thumb (if you've got a small thumb). Dennis pointed his blaster at Walter, pulled the trigger and... his elbow dribbled.

Walter laughed and SPLOOOSH! he squirted Dennis again! SPLOOOSH!

Where was Gnasher? Dennis ran back inside. He found his best friend lying, spread out, on the sofa. *He's given up on me*, thought Dennis. *How can Gnasher still think I'm amazing, with such a high fail rate?*

***

Now here Dennis was, in the back garden, without his skateboard or his best friend by his side. *How can this day get any worse?* he thought.

LA, LA, LA!
I'M NOT LISTENING!

Gran was one of Dennis's favourite people. She was definitely his favourite grown-up. He did love his mum and dad, but they were too judgy. They'd say things like, "How long's that lolly been stuck in your hair?" and, "Stop painting that word on the lawn!" and, "What's that doing in your hand?! It should be attached to the car!"

Stuff like that.

But Gran was different. She wasn't like other grown-ups. She seemed to think he was just right the way he was.

And now she was in hospital.

Dennis dove into the back of the car, while his parents clambered into the front.

"What's happened?" Dennis asked.

Dad slammed the car into reverse and backed out of the drive faster than he ever had before,

causing a passing ice-cream van to swerve and crash into the lamp post across the road.

"She's fallen and done her hip in!" Dad said as he crunched and forced the gears into forwards. Then he burned off up the road for six seconds, before suddenly stopping with a massive skid.

"Why are you...?" Mum started to ask, before remembering the same thing Dad had remembered. **"The baby!"**

Dad slammed the car back into reverse and floored it until, three seconds later, they were back home. Mum piled back into the house, realising they'd left the front door wide open, scooped up Dennis's little sister, Bea, in her arms and ran back out, closing the door this time and locking it, too.

***

Dennis didn't like hospitals. They were boring. There was always a lot of waiting.

There was waiting that time he'd swallowed that penny.

Waiting that time he'd broken his arm.

Waiting that time he re-swallowed the penny he'd kept as a souvenir after they'd sucked it out of him that first time (he'd swallowed it deliberately, showing his mate Pieface how he'd accidentally swallowed it the first time).

This time, though, the hospital didn't have the boring waiting. They just went straight to Gran's ward to see her. It's a shame Dad didn't see Gran first, actually, because when he stepped out of the lift she crashed into him in her wheelchair.

"Arrrgh!" Gran shouted. "Watch it, you big idiot! I've done my hip in, you know."

"I know!" Dad said, nursing his bruised shin. "You told me in a text, remember?"

She turned and started wheeling herself up the corridor towards her ward, one leg pointing out in front of her like a foot-shaped battering ram.

Dad followed. "Is it broken?"

"Nope," Gran called over her shoulder. "They thought it was, but it's actually just badly bruised."

Gran swept into the ward and expertly parked her wheelchair next to her bed, like she'd been using a wheelchair all her life.

"And how did you do it?" Dad asked.

"I fell off my skateboard," Gran answered.

Dad's eyes widened. "You don't have a skateboard. What have you got a skateboard for? You're eighty!"

Gran pulled a battered, well-worn skateboard out of the cupboard next to the bed. "I don't know. I don't remember getting it."

"That's **Dennis's** skateboard!" Mum cried.

Then a few of Dennis's memories reordered themselves. After Mum had thrown his board out of the kitchen window and into the back garden,

Dennis had gone over to Gran's. He'd been hoping to hear one of those stories about Dad when he was his age and got in trouble as much as Dennis does now... and for biscuits. Gran's biscuit tin was amazing. Everything in there was covered in thick chocolate and wrapped in foil. Like those biscuits that are in the house during the first half of Christmas Day but at Gran's it was all year round.

He must have left his skateboard there by accident. The glares off Dad and Mum were proper harsh, as Dennis would say. Judging by her frown, even little Bea was laying on the guilt. Either that or she was doing a poo.

It wasn't right to blame Dennis for this! He'd just left it round her house. It wasn't like he'd made Gran get on the board.

Suddenly, another memory slotted into place. "Why don't you have a go, Gran?" he remembered saying. "I'll show you how to do a kickflip!" Dennis winced at the memory.

But Gran seemed to have forgotten both that and him lending his skateboard to her 'for practice'.

"They want to keep me in overnight," she said. "Some nonsense about sometimes a bone doesn't look broken but later turns out it is, or something. Personally, I think the doctor just fancies me."

Dad put his fingers in his ears and shouted, **"La, La, La! I'm not listening!"**

The car journey home wasn't fun. Time and again, Mum and Dad pointed out how fragile old ladies were, and how it didn't matter that Gran did

karate and rock climbing and dirt biking, she was still eighty.

In the back seat, Dennis tried to sink as low as he could, but it wasn't low enough. He attempted to lighten the mood and look on the positive side by saying, "At least I got my board back!" But somehow that seemed to make things worse.

And worse even than that, earlier on, Bea's frown had been because she *was* doing a poo. The stench from the nappy was unbelievable!

"**Arrrgh!** Open the windows," Dad shouted.

"It's so bad, I can taste it with my *eyeballs*!" Dennis cried.

Back home, Dennis was sent to his room and because it was that serious, the Wi-Fi was turned off, too. He lay on his bed in a low, confused funk. He felt bad for Gran. He'd never wish any sort of badness on her, but was it his fault? Did she blame him? That was the question. She didn't even seem to remember that it was his skateboard.

Dumb, stupid, boring emotions were dumb, stupid and boring! Happy, angry, bored and hungry were the only emotions he knew how to cope with. This guilt thing was the worst feeling yet. He had to sort it out. He decided that in the morning he'd go and see Gran. To see if they were still cool.

QUAD BIKES ARE COOLER

The next morning, Dennis got up even before Bea had started wailing to have her latest guff-tastically gross nappy changed. He tiptoed downstairs and collected his skateboard from the shoe cupboard where Mum had banished it. He tried to get Gnasher to come with him, but the dog just ignored him and carried on sleeping in the kitchen. Gnasher still thought Dennis was awesome. He didn't think he'd lost any of his core Dennisness, but it was Sunday morning!

Having quietly escaped the house and skated to the hospital, and having been told once by a security guard at the hospital to stop skating, Dennis made his way back to Gran's ward.

Cautiously, he poked his head round the corner, saw Gran, who was now lying in bed, and sheepishly said, "Hi, Gran. How are you?"

Gran looked up from her tablet device and

smiled. "Oh, hi Dennis! What are you doing back here? And so early in the morning?"

He looked at her guiltily.

"Your parents gave you a hard time when they found out it was your board," Gran guessed. "They shouldn't have. It's not your fault. It's mine."

"I know! *Totally* your fault!" Dennis exclaimed. "But let's not blame anyone," he added.

"I'd forgotten it was your board," Gran continued. "I used to have one in the '70s, you see but I'm not as steady on my pins as I was. I'm even thinking of switching my dirt bike for a quad bike."

"I think quad bikes are cooler," Dennis reassured her.

Dennis's mood had lifted, but only slightly. Gran sensed that something still wasn't quite right.

"I sense that something still isn't quite right," she said.

Dennis sat in Gran's wheelchair and stuck his leg up on the thingy to rest busted-up legs on, then sighed.

"I've run out of awesomeness, or something, Gran," he said. "Used it all up. I'm not surprised. I've been completely awesome and totally brilliant since I was born. A hundred per cent, all the time."

"And you're really modest, too," Gran interjected with a smile.

"Yeah, modest! Proper modest!" Dennis agreed, without knowing what modest even meant. "I thought I had infinite awesomeness, but now it's gone. My tricks aren't working and my pranks are backfiring. I reckon Gnasher even senses I'm out of juice now, because he's not bothering with me any more, either..."

"I don't think you've run out of awesomeness," Gran told Dennis. "It's town-wide. Haven't you noticed how boring everything's become lately? The town elephant hasn't escaped for weeks. There's usually a tanker full of custard crashing into a truck full of mince pies or the fizzy-pop factory exploding every other day or something. Beanotown's gone..."

"The town's gone what?" asked Dennis.

"I was pausing for dramatic effect!" said Gran.

"Well, is the dramatic pause over yet?" Dennis asked. "I don't have all day!"

"Beanotown's gone normal. Completely and **horribly** average!" Gran shouted.

She paused again. This time for thought.

"This happened in Beanotown once before," she said.

"When?" asked Dennis. "Why?"

"There's no way to tell that story without also telling my own," Gran said cryptically. "It was whatever year it was 70 years ago..."

Dennis was already hooked. *This is going to be awesome!* he thought.

"I was very much like you," she continued, "but a girl."

Suddenly, everything around Dennis started going all wibbly-wobbly and Dennis heard some twinkly music.

"**Arrrgh!** What's happening?" he shouted.

"Chill out," Gran advised. "It's a flashback.
Just go with it."

THIS IS BASH STREET!

When Gran was ten, seventy years ago, Gran wasn't called Gran. She was called Catherine. Katie, for short. And seventy years ago, Katie was bored. She sat with the same menace scowl that Dennis thought he'd invented and shouted **"I'm bored!"** at the rest of the plane.

Didn't I mention she was on a plane?

She was on an old Bristol Type 130 Bombay, but this was shortly after World War II, when such

bombers were relatively new. The school had bought it from the Royal Air Force the year before, refitted it in metalwork class and repainted it, in the school colours, in Art.

Katie and the rest of her Geography class were currently flying over the Amazon rainforest...

***

"Hold on! Hold on! Wait. Time out," Dennis interrupted. "You were in a what? Over where!?"

"You're spoiling the flashback!" Gran sulked.

"The school bought a plane and the kids did it up, and you went out on school trips to the Amazon in it!?"

"It was a different time back then," Gran informed him. "These days, they won't let you shoot kids out of a cannon into the sea without filling out a form. It's health and safety gone mad, I tell you! Back then, things were much more relaxed. Anyway, where was I? Oh yeah, we were out over the Amazon..."

"Catherine Menace!" Mr Teacherson said, his fists resting on his hips, in that way he always did. "This is Geography! It's not meant to be 'fun' or 'exciting'. It's meant to be Geography!"

Katie leant back against the side of the plane and started picking at a little patch of tin riveted over one of the bullet holes (the school had bought the plane cheap, as it was full of bullet holes).

"When are we going to jump, sir?" she asked.

"All in good time, young lady," Mr Teacherson blustered. "It's almost as if you're not interested in how oxbow lakes are formed!"

* * *

"Hold on! Wait!" Dennis interrupted again. "You were getting ready to jump? Out of a plane! Over the Amazon! In Geography!"

"Are you going to interrupt every two minutes?" Gran asked.

"Yes, I think I am." Dennis replied.

"Well, don't! You're ruining my flow," Gran told him. "Save all your 'Hold on! Wait!'s till the end or I'll never get through it. Er... so blah-blah, plane, Amazon, oxbow lakes..."

* * *

Katie rolled her eyes. "Can't we do something interesting, like look for Cringebeard's treasure, or his Pea-shooter of Everlasting Fun or something?" she asked.

"The legend of Cringebeard's treasure is a load of absolute **nonsense!**" Mr Teacherson shouted over the noise of the propellers. "How does a pirate get this far south? The Caribbean is 600 miles north of here!"

"Down through the Orinoco River," Katie answered. "Then through the Casiquiare canal, sir. That's connected to the Amazon," Katie finished with a huge grin.

But Mr Teacherson was looking angrily out of the window.

"**Grrrah!**" he shouted. "We've missed the oxbow lake now! Everybody out! **Go! Go! Go!**"

Quickly, the class all ran to the open hatch and leapt out of the plane. All except the new pupil, Leonardo McGlinchy, who stopped before he jumped, and Catherine who was stuck waiting impatiently behind him.

"I can't go!" shouted McGlinchy. "Does this not seem like a dangerous thing for schoolkids to do? We've hardly had any training!"

"What are you talking about? We had a whole PE lesson about it on Tuesday," Katie reminded McGlinchy.

"I was *ill* on Tuesday!" McGlinchy pointed out, though he wasn't sure anyone was really listening.

Catherine thought Leonardo McGlinchy was dreamy. His hair was especially dreamy, but he could be a bit of a scaredy-cat sometimes. Take swimming, for instance. He thought the children should learn to swim in a swimming pool and not be blasted out of a cannon into the sea.

"You're not at that posh school now, McGlinchy," Katie shouted. "This is **Bash Street!**" And she kicked him out of the plane.

THE SHOOTY END

It was a simpler time back then, where if a girl kicked you out of a plane, it meant she fancied you... or really wanted you to get out of a plane.

Katie landed perfectly and removed her parachute, just like she'd been taught in PE, but McGlinchy ended up stuck in a tree. Helpful as ever, Katie climbed up and cut him down. After he fell to the jungle floor, she dropped down next to him and gave him a dead arm.

"**Ow!**" he shouted. "What was that for?"

"We're miles from the drop zone now, because of you not getting out when everyone else did," Katie shouted back. "We'll have to find our own way. It could take **weeks!**"

"Well, excuse me for thinking ten-year-olds shouldn't jump out of planes into jungles," McGlinchy huffed.

Katie scowled.

"What's that scowl all about, Katie?"
McGlinchy asked.

"It's the Menace family scowl," she explained,
scowling even deeper.

"The Menace family scowl?" He looked completely confused.

"Yes. I'm a Menace and this is how us Menaces scowl." Why did she like him? He was an idiot.

Seeing that he was still confused, she dropped the scowl and turned away.

"Just follow me!" she said, looking back. "And watch where you're walking."

With a purposeful step, she fell down the gaping hole in front of her.

"Katie!" McGlinchy shouted down into the hole. "Are you okay?"

At the bottom of the hole, Katie lay on the damp moss-covered ground thinking that she didn't like Geography.

"I'm fine!" she shouted back, feeling around in her pocket for her torch.

She turned it on and pointed it around the cave in which she now found herself. Quickly, the torchlight caught a glint of something buried in the wall. Katie crawled over and dug it out then held it close to her face for inspection.

"Come down here," she called up to McGlinchy. "I've found something."

She held up a golden doubloon.

"Pirate treasure!" McGlinchy cried, getting down on all fours and peering over the edge.

"I can't see a way out," Katie observed. "Dangle one of those vines down here or..."

Straining to hear her, McGlinchy leaned further over the edge... and fell down into the hole next to her.

"... Or we'll never get out!" Katie finished.

"The edge of that hole is dangerous!" McGlinchy said, looking up at Katie. "There should be a sign, or a railing."

Katie threw the gold coin at him.

"Here you go," she said. "Buy a railing. Now, let's see if we can find another way out of here. It actually looks like quite a big cave."

As they moved deeper into it they found more and more coins, until the floor was littered, then covered, with gold. Their minds boggled. Oh! the things they could do with it.

A fart-powered hoverboard, thought Katie, her eyes sparkling at the prospect of the trouble she could cause in Beanotown.

Investments, mused McGlinchy, sensibly.

They waded knee-deep in doubloons until, finally, they came upon a skeleton. He was dressed in the finest pirate gear, sitting on a golden throne. In one bony hand he held what could only be described as a fancy golden pea-shooter. At one end it had a

mouthpiece similar to that of a trumpet and near the shooty end was a sight.

"Incredible! This must be Cringebeard's Golden Pea-shooter of Everlasting Fun!" McGlinchy exclaimed in awe.

Katie snatched the Pea-shooter from him.

"Whoa!" she said. "I can feel the power of this thing!"

She picked a little stone out of the wall, put it in the Pea-shooter and blew. Never before in the history of stuff getting shot from pea-shooters did anything fly so straight and true.

The little pebble pinged off the left wall, pinged off the right wall. PING, PING, PING! all the way down the cave. It hit a rock on the floor near where they fell down, then pinged up out into the jungle, hit a vine and knocked it loose. The vine dropped down into the cave... the perfect way out.

"Come on!" Katie said. "Let's take this back with us to Beanotown."

McGlinchy wasn't so sure. "But this is Cringebeard's final resting place."

"So?" asked Katie. "He's not using it."

"It's his tomb! Are you seriously suggesting we raid his tomb? That would make us—"

"Tomb raiders?" said Katie, finishing his thought. "I'm cool with that." She took a step back towards the cave entrance.

Suddenly, a powerful wind rose up and blew around the cave, accompanied by a terrible roar. The skeleton moved.

"It's just the wind," she said.

But when the skeleton got up and grabbed Katie, it was pretty obvious that it was a bit more than that.

The skull tipped back and the jaw dropped down as the ex-pirate began to glow. In the eye sockets, glowing liquid pooled and turned white, transforming into eyes. While this happened, the glowing chin sprouted hair, which grew and grew until seconds later, the hair was as long as any pirate captain's beard. In its mouth a tongue formed and the skull began to scream. The kids screamed, too. Well, wouldn't you?

If there are any parents reading this, it was like that bit in a film you take your kids to, thinking it's going to be perfectly acceptable for children,

only to have something a bit too scary happen a third of the way in. You know, just before you look to your little darling to check they're okay and you see they're loving it.

Then Cringebeard burst out laughing. "Haw! Haw! Haw!" he laughed. "Your faces! Wish I had a camera. Cameras have been invented by now, yeah?"

The children looked at one another in disbelief. Cringebeard was haunting his own skeleton!

Suddenly, Cringebeard flipped into angry ghost mode.

"**Steal from me** would you?!"

Cringebeard rose up and began to float. The terrible wind returned and whirled around the cavern. Gold coins were picked up, flying around and around the terrifying piratical figure. The children cowered; McGlinchy nearly fainted.

"Good for you!" Cringebeard boomed. Then he laughed again as the wind stopped and all the coins dropped out of the air.

Katie and McGlinchy gave each other that 'Huh?' look.

"I'm a **pirate**, ya noggins!" Cringebeard told them. "All the treasure 'ere was stolen an' this is only half of what I used to have." The ghostly pirate lowered back down and said in a quieter voice, "Do you know why?"

"Er... because it was stolen?" asked Katie.

Cringebeard laughed again. A big, booming laugh. "Yes! By my mum. Bless her twisted soul. She said I owed her for all the free dinners and clothes I got as a little 'un. That pea-shooter there was one of me toys when I were a kid. My dear old ma stole the golden idol of the magic Pranky monkey god from the lost tribe of mountain jokers," said Cringebeard. "She melted it down and made a pea-shooter for me out of it."

"The Pranky monkey god?" Katie asked.

The spectral stealer shrugged. "The thing does have power, somehow. It's no ordinary gold."

"So... we can really take this, can we?" Katie asked nervously.

"Sure! It's yours. I don't need it. Now that I'm dead, I have my own powers," the ex-pirate replied. "But ten years from now I will have me **revenge!**" he shouted as the wind picked up again and he rose up into the air once more.

Then, two seconds later, it stopped when the pirate started laughing again.

"Haw! Haw! Haw! Your faces, honestly. Go on. Off with you!"

* * *

"And that's the story of how I got Cringebeard's fabled Golden Pea-shooter of Everlasting Fun," Gran grinned, lying back in bed. "And pockets full of doubloons."

"But you were meant to be telling me about the last time the town went boring."

"Was I?" asked Gran, looking slightly puzzled. "Why did I tell you about the Pea-shooter, then?"

"How should I know!" Dennis shouted, throwing his hands up.

Gran thought again.

"Okay. I think I got it," Gran answered, "but it will have to wait until the next chapter..."

IN TROUBLE AGAIN, OR STILL IN TROUBLE?

"The next chapter?" Dennis asked. "What's that meant to mean?"

"It doesn't mean anything now," said Gran. "So, McGlinchy and I climbed out of Cringebeard's cave and set off home. After six days in the jungle, we found a fisherman who took us to Macapá. There, we stowed away on a steamer to French Guiana. In

French Guiana, we stowed away on another ship bound for the British Virgin Islands.

To cut a long story short, five weeks later we were home. Your great-grandma was furious. She'd made my dinner five weeks ago and by then it was stone cold.

At school, though, McGlinchy and I could prank no wrong. Filled with the power of the Golden Pea-shooter, things from our catapults always found their targets. Water bombs hit home. That thing where you put something on top of a door before someone walks in always worked. It was a wonderful time." She paused for thought.

"If you blew through it, whatever was in front of you would have an accident or something funny would happen to it. I blew it at a truck full of bouncy balls once and it crashed into the railings on a bridge, and all the balls spilled out and bounced all over town!" Gran exploded in a fit of giggles. It took a moment before she was able to continue.

"It wasn't just us. All our friends experienced the same, as though simply having the Pea-shooter close by gave us all special pranking powers. We were simply unstoppable."

"Stop!" Dennis shouted. "You're doing it again. I'm loving the sound of this Pea-shooter," he said angrily, "but you're meant to be explaining how the town got boring last time."

"Stick with me," Gran assured Dennis, "it's connected... Then, one day, Mr Teacherson caught me with the Pea-shooter and because they were banned in school, he confiscated it. It was a surprise, but not a huge disaster until I broke into the confiscation cupboard just a few minutes later and it wasn't there!"

"It had *disappeared*? What did you do, Gran?" Dennis asked.

"I heard a rumour it had surfaced in Egypt, but that turned out to be the Golden Spear of Tep. Then I heard it'd been found at the South Pole, in the Mountains of Badness, but that was just the Golden Bow of Blerrak-ak-ak. McGlinchy and I spent every doubloon we had going all over the world in search of the Golden Pea-shooter. We even went to Wigan! But all we found there was the Golden Pie of Sir Noms-a-lot."

Gran sat back.

"The one thing I could never figure out is how we got caught with it in the first place. We had the power of the Golden Pea-shooter! We were untouchable. Mr Teacherson shouldn't have been able to catch us."

Gran shook her head.

"That was the start of the boring," Gran continued. "It's hard to explain quite how boring things got back then. I mean, how do you describe **nothing** happening? But nothing did happen. Nothing whatsoever. For days..."

"Don't dramatic pause," Dennis told Gran, "just keep going."

"Well," said Gran. "One boring thing that happened was a school History trip to the museum–"

"I like the dinosaur bit in the museum," Dennis interrupted.

"This was a trip to see the parts of the museum that didn't have dinosaurs," Gran told him.

Dennis gasped in horror.

"It was while we were at the museum I saw the latest exhibit. The Golden Yawning Penguin of Boringness!"

"Finally!" Dennis exclaimed. "How long's this taken?" He looked at his wrist, where there would be a watch if he had one. "Am I still ten?"

"I read the little bit of paper that was under the exhibit, explaining what it was, and it said...

The Golden Yawning
Penguin of Boringness.
340 BC
This gold statue once belonged to a lost tribe of teachers from deepest Yawntopia and is said to have sinister powers.

"Well, it was obvious to me that this thing was the cause of the trouble," Gran said. "Magic boredom penguin, new to the museum. Had to be. So I nicked it."

Dennis's eyes widened so much they nearly fell out.

"I grabbed it. The thing was shaking and vibrating in my arms. It felt like it was going to explode or something any second, but I ran out of there. All the way to the swimming cannon, with museum guards and Mr Teacherson chasing me every step of the way."

"Swimming cannon?" Dennis asked.

"Remember," Gran reminded Dennis, "back in the last chapter, when I told you that kids learnt how to swim by being shot out of a cannon into the sea. Anyway, I got to the swimming cannon, loaded the Penguin into it, and shot it out to sea. I had the cannon turned up to full power, so it went for miles. Right over the horizon."

"**Wow!** What happened next?" asked Dennis. "Did you find the Pea-shooter again?"

"Everything went back to normal in Beanotown. Well, I say 'normal'. That day, all the extraordinariness seemed to come back at once. Normally, it's only the elephant that escapes the safari park. But that day somehow every animal escaped at the same time. Mass breakout! A dinosaur also escaped from Duck Island. Big hairy thing it was. Looked a bit like Gnasher. The main jam pipeline into town burst, flooding the precinct with strawberry jam. There was a candyfloss machine outside the amusements back then. Lightning hit it and created a candyfloss monster..."

"Cool!"

"That wasn't the half of it. Eventually it calmed down though and went back to normal. Well, normal by Beanotown standards anyway."

Gran narrowed her eyes and thought.

"Thinking about it now, it was almost as if the Penguin had been holding back the fun and weirdness of the town. And it built up. So when the Penguin was gone, there was a flood of weirdness."

"Do you think the Golden Yawning Penguin of Boringness has returned?" Dennis asked.

"Yes," replied Gran very seriously.

"Then I know what I must do!" Dennis exclaimed, leaping from the wheelchair.

"Great! You need to find the Penguin and get it out of town."

"No!" Dennis disagreed. "I need to find the Golden Pea-shooter."

"But you need to find the Penguin and get rid of it!"

"Naw," said Dennis. "My plan's better."

"What plan?" Gran asked.

"To get the Pea-shooter and, you know, whatever, and that," Dennis informed her.

"That's not a plan!" Gran said.

But it was all the planning Dennis ever did. He didn't even bother calling it Plan A – his plans were so quickly formed there wasn't time to stick a letter in front of them.

"Gran, is there anywhere you *didn't* look for the Golden Pea-shooter?"

"We looked everywhere," Gran answered.

"Absolutely everywhere?"

"Yes."

"Absolutely, totally everywhere?"

"Yes!"

"Absolutely, totally, positively everywhere? Even in Beanotown?"

Gran narrowed her eyes. "Oh, now that would be annoying..."

***

Dennis left the hospital with a spring in his step, which was useful for all the kickflips he did on the way home. The Golden Pea-shooter was in Beanotown! Dennis was sure of it.

"Gnasher!" Dennis called out as he walked through the front door.

Suddenly, it all kicked off. Dad was really angry for some reason.

"You're meant to be **in your room!**" he shouted as soon as he saw Dennis.

"Why?" Dennis asked, what was he in trouble for this time?

"Because you put Gran in the **hospital!**"

Dennis's head was full of magical golden objects, but he quickly remembered the bit of

trouble leading up to the cool bit about ghost pirates. He wasn't in trouble again, this was the trouble he was in from before. The same trouble.

"Hey! That was **nothing** to do with me," Dennis shouted back. "Gran says it was her fault. I've just come from there."

That didn't help and Dennis found himself banished to his room again, with the Wi-Fi turned off, again.

The word egregious (egg-ree-gee-uss) means extraordinarily bad or shocking. If Dennis had known that, he would have said it was egregious.

"This is lame, Gnasher!" he said to Gnasher as Gnasher licked his face. "At least you're back to liking me."

Gnasher thought this was a bit of a weird thing to say. When had he stopped?

***

Getting this sort of information out of Gnasher was tricky. In the first interview with him for this book, I asked him, "Why did Dennis think you had in some way gone off him, or thought he was no longer cool?"

"Gnash, Gnash Gnash, Gnash," said Gnasher.

"I see. Have the two of you ever had a real falling-out?"

"Gnash, Gnash Gnash, Gnash Gnash Gnash!" Gnasher answered.

"Right. I see..."

My research wasn't going well. It took a trip to Beanotown's top-secret research station, and weeks of work with the scientists there, to develop a dog translator. We aptly named it the Gnash-Gnash Mark One.

***

That night, Dennis fell into a fitful sleep. He dreamt of the challenges and dangers that lay before him. None of it could be true.

Or could it?

No. It couldn't.

But could it, though?

No. Probably not.

Yeah, but could it, though?

Maybe.

ENTER THE MINX!

The next morning was Monday, but it wasn't one of those rubbish Monday mornings when you had to go to school. It was some sort of holiday or something. Dennis's cousin Minnie didn't ask what. The only information she needed was that she didn't have to go to school.

Minnie, more commonly known as Minnie the Minx, stepped out of her house ready to meet the day head-on.

"... And **stay out** till dinner time!" her mother shouted from inside.

Minnie rolled her eyes. You put one tiny crack in one little vase and that's it. One tiny little total-smash-of-the-vase-with-a-cricket-bat and suddenly you're the bad guy! Only the vase was actually the new telly.

"You're being **egregious!**" Minnie shouted right back at her.

Inside the house, Mum grabbed the 'word of the day' calendar, which was displaying the word of the day, 'egregious', and flicked ahead.

Innocuous? No.

Convivial? No.

Jocose? No.

Then Mum found something, four days from now, that fit.

"Yes? Well, you're **vexatious!**" Minnie's mum shouted back.

But by this time Minnie was out of earshot.

Mum was being unfair, Minnie thought. The whole cricket-bat-plus-TV thing was only partly her fault. If you don't want cricket bat-related issues in the house, don't have a cricket bat in the house.

It's that simple.

Yes, technically Minnie had been the one to bring the bat into the house in the first place, if you wanted to get bogged down in pointless details, but Minnie was never one for stressing on the details.

Over the road, Minnie spotted Dennis and Gnasher. Dennis looked like he was trying really hard to think.

Because Dennis's thinking usually led to something interesting (trouble), Minnie crossed to get involved and see if she could make the situation what she would call better but most grown-ups might call worse.

"Get lost, Minnie!" Dennis shouted as soon as he saw her. "I don't have time to deal with whatever destruction you're going to cause. I'm on a very important mission."

Minnie was offended. "I'll have you know I've already destroyed the thing I was going to destroy, before I even got thrown out of the house. I'm here to help. Minnie and Dennis! It'll be like an all-action crossover," she said, doing some karate kicks and chops in the air.

"This is not the sort of thing that needs your brand of chaos," Dennis said. "I'm looking for a weird, old thing."

"This weird, old thing," Minnie wondered. "Is it weird?"

"Yes."

"And is this weird old thing also old?"

Dennis's eyes lit up. "Yes, it is. How did you know that?"

"Well then," said Minnie matter-of-factly. "I think we should start by looking in a place that's full of weird, old things."

"The museum!" Dennis cried. "Of course!" and he and Gnasher ran off up the street.

"Well, I was thinking the teachers' room at school, but whatever," said Minnie and followed.

Dennis, Gnasher and Minnie ran into the museum at top speed, only to be stopped by some loser before they even got as far as the first dinosaur.

"No running in the museum!" the loser said, standing in front of them with his hands out in a classic 'halt' pose.

"Where's your old stuff?" Dennis asked.

"You're in a museum," said the also old museum curator. "A lot of the exhibits here are old."

"Well, where's the weird stuff, then?" Dennis tried again.

The curator looked round at the cyclops skeleton, the Viking steam-powered robot, Thor's Toothpick of Justice, the six-horned triceratops skull, the Mitten of Doom, the time machine, the other time machine, the crystal skull, the iron skull,

73

the custard skull, *The Book of Everything*, the Jade Cat of Indifference, the Little Yellow Elephant of Truth, the Spoon of Hope, the 6th-century hamster armour, the Sholupog of Blergshmoo, the Shoe of Hope...

"It's all weird!" the curator replied. Dennis read the name on the curator's badge.

MITTEN OF DOOM

74

"Listen up, McGlinchy. We're looking for Cringebeard's Golden Pea-shooter of Everlasting Fun," Dennis said.

Suddenly, they both staggered back and gasped. Dennis at realising the museum curator was Gran's schoolfriend McGlinchy. McGlinchy at hearing that someone was looking for Cringebeard's Golden Pea-shooter of Everlasting Fun.

And it was a big gasp. It went on for ages. As long as it took you to read from 'suddenly they both staggered back and gasped' up to here.

That long.

"What do you want with Cringebeard's Golden Pea-shooter of Everlasting Fun?" asked the old man, feeling a bit dizzy from the gasp.

"I need to charge up my awesomeness or menace, or whatever it is that makes me so amazing, normally," Dennis replied.

"And what about you?" the curator asked Minnie. "Why are you here?"

"I broke a telly," Minnie answered.

"Enough about us," said Dennis. "What do you know about the Pea-shooter? Spill!"

"Well," said the old man, "there's no way to tell the story of Cringebeard's Golden Pea-shooter of Everlasting Fun without also telling my own..."

Suddenly, everything around Dennis, Gnasher and Minnie started going all wibbly-wobbly, and they heard some twinkly music.

Dennis jumped forwards, waving his arms. "**Stop! Stop! Stop!** We're not having another flashback. Even if it is from a different point of view."

The man peered closely at Dennis and a look of recognition came over him. "You're Dennis! You're Katie's grandson! I've seen pictures of you on her Facebook page. We used to be friends at school, once upon a time. We haven't actually talked since then, but we friended each other a while back. How is she?"

"She's in hospital. She tried to kickflip my skateboard and did her hip in."

McGlinchy looked worried. "Was anyone watching? Was it hilarious?" he asked.

"No!" Dennis took offence on Gran' behalf. "She was on her own and she really hurt herself."

"Then it *is* back," McGlinchy said to himself.

"The Yawning Golden Penguin of Boringness," said Dennis. "I know. I'm not interested in that, I want the Pea-shooter."

"Hey! Hold on. Penguins aren't boring. They're cool! Literally, figuratively and in actuality," Minnie said.

Dennis looked at Minnie in disbelief.

"We've got a fancy 'word of the day' calendar in our house," said Minnie. "Mum thought it'd be good to improve my vocabulary, but I've been using it to wind her up with fancy words."

"Yes, real penguins are cool, in both senses," McGlinchy agreed, "but this is just a little gold

statue. Not a real one. And it
radiates boringness. That's why
your Gran got caught with
the Pea-shooter... it was
when the Penguin arrived.

"It was lucky, really.
Katie had started to act
strangely. Not like herself.
I mean, she was always
all action, and never
really worried about what
might go wrong, but since
getting the Pea-shooter,
she'd changed. Her pranks were getting out of hand.
Dangerous to herself and others."

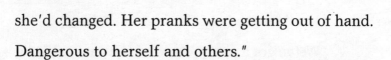

Dennis remembered Gran telling him in the
hospital about the time she used the Pea-shooter to
make a truck full of bouncy balls crash. Thinking
about it now, that was a bit much. Someone could
have easily been hurt and that wasn't like Gran.

"So I broke into the confiscation cupboard, took the Pea-shooter and hid it in the caves under the museum. When I left school I managed to get a job here so I could keep an eye on it... I stayed here so long I ended up running the place."

"You!" Dennis pointed at McGlinchy. "You took the Pea-shooter! **You betrayed Gran!**"

"Plot twist!" said Minnie, munching on some popcorn she'd somehow got from somewhere.

"I didn't betray her!" said McGlinchy. "I was trying to protect her. She was always doing dangerous stuff. She may not have been that into me, but I loved her."

McGlinchy didn't like the way Dennis was looking at him. He was the hero!

In Cringebeard's cave, if you remember, McGlinchy had been against them taking the Pea-shooter. At the time, he'd made it sound like it wasn't a good idea to become a tomb raider, but really he wasn't that bothered about that. He was doing what he could to keep Katie safe.

"She loved you too, you idiot," Dennis cried.

"No she didn't," McGlinchy said. "She kicked me out of a plane!"

"If I liked a boy, I'd kick him out of a plane," Minnie commented. "Just saying." And with that she stuffed another handful of popcorn into her mouth.

"You loved her because she was *her*!" Dennis said. "Doing dangerous stuff is what she does."

"**Urrrgh!** Whatever!" McGlinchy shouted, throwing up his hands. "It doesn't matter now. It was all so long ago. I suppose you're here to get the Golden Pea-shooter so you can find the Penguin?"

"Er... will finding one help me track down the other?" Dennis asked.

"Perhaps," McGlinchy said. "The boring of the Penguin and the excitement of the Pea-shooter push against each other, but the power of prankiness is stronger. I remember Katie telling me that when she picked up the Penguin it was shaking like it was going to explode. I have a theory that the Pea-shooter may be able to overcome the Penguin. We don't know where in town the Penguin is exactly, but if

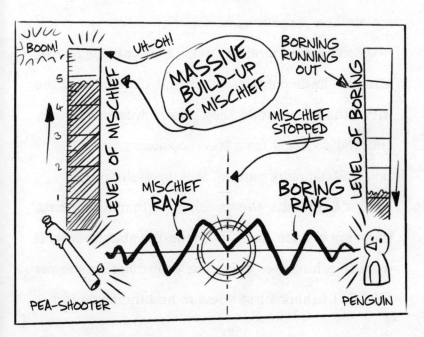

you travel round town with the Pea-shooter, I think you'll be able to tell from the resistance between them. And if you get the Pea-shooter near enough to the Penguin, I think you can destroy it."

"Perfect!" Dennis announced. "Because that was my plan all along," he fibbed.

"This is where it gets tricky," said McGlinchy. "The Pea-shooter is in the Chamber of Mischief."

"Chamber of Mischief?" Dennis and Minnie repeated together.

"Yes," explained McGlinchy. "Over the years, to keep it safe, I've built a... well, a series of chambers, actually. Each contains traps and challenges more tricky than the last, to keep prying eyes – especially children's – away from the Pea-shooter."

McGlinchy paused, looking guilty.

"But that's the problem with magic items. They affect each other. Like the Pea-shooter affects the Penguin. I was trying to keep the Pea-shooter safe. But I think I put a few too many magic things down there... It's sort of got out of hand. I'm not sure anyone would be able to make it through now."

McGlinchy was bright red, and looked like he wanted to curl up and hide in a corner.

"Where is this chamber?" Dennis asked.

"The entrance is in the Middle Ages." He turned and began to walk briskly away. "I've got, er, you know... museum stuff to do. Totally not running away because I'm scared. Definitely not that!"

Then, he remembered: *That's the second time this week someone's come asking about that.*

WHERE TO GO IF ZOMBIES EVER START BEING A THING

Dennis and Minnie trudged off into the Middle Ages. Not the actual Middle Ages – the bit of the museum that was about the Middle Ages.

"All this stuff that's not dinosaurs is boring," Dennis complained.

Minnie liked museums. Even the bits that didn't have dinosaurs. There're the bits with Vikings and other warriors, for example. Armour, weapons. If zombies ever started being a thing, Minnie was going to head straight to the museum.

From the stuff in the display cases, the children agreed that from AD 500 to AD 1500 – i.e. the Middle Ages – things were pretty yawn-some. Not much was invented. It seemed to be before or after cool stuff happened.

Searching the museum, they were hoping to find the entrance to the Chamber of Mischief. They were definitely not looking for Walter. Walter was the last thing they were looking for.

They bumped into Walter.

"**Urrrgh!** What are you two doing here?" Walter asked, looking hugely disappointed. "This is a museum, you know. If you're not careful, you two might learn something!"

Dennis, Gnasher and Minnie rolled their eyes.

Walter looked around. "Interested in the Middle Ages, are you? They were quite a time," he said, going all misty-eyed about history's most boring bit.

"Quite a lot of disease back then, but they knew how to keep order. You'd have been clapped in irons back in those days, Dennis, and I'm pretty sure they would have burnt you at the stake, Minnie."

"Too right they would have tried!" Minnie answered. "I'd have been an awesome, hideous witch. They'd have got me and tied me to the stake and then, just as the flames got dead big, I'd have

magicked away the rope, flown up into the air and
zapped them all into frogs!"

"No you wouldn't!" Walter complained.
"Witches weren't real. They didn't have evil powers."

"I did!" Minnie retorted. "I had amazing
powers and I zapped every last one of them. They're
still frogs now."

Minnie was now talking as if she had actually
been a witch in the Middle Ages and it was hard to
tell if she believed that or not.

"We're getting off track!" Dennis cried.
"We're not here for whatever this is. We're here for
the Chamber of Mischief."

"Chamber of Mischief?" Walter asked.

"Chamber of Get-lost Walter!" Minnie snapped back.

"It's here!" said Dennis, running over to a small, unassuming door between the display cases.

Actually, it wasn't even small. It was just door-sized. It was just a door-sized wooden door the size of a door. On the door was a small sign: 'Chamber of Mischief. No Entry.'

"Y-you can't go in th-there! It says 'no entry'," Walter stammered, as if that meant something.

Dennis walked over to the world's most ordinary door and opened it. Walter gasped in horror at someone doing what a sign said not to.

"Whoa!" Walter shouted. "What are you doing? It says, 'No Entry'!"

"Stop being you!" Dennis said, and went inside. He wasn't going to let a little thing like a sign stop him. He had to get that Pea-shooter so he didn't end up average. He was followed by Gnasher, Minnie and Walter.

"Why are you following us?" asked Dennis. "I thought 'No Entry' was a massive deal."

"You opened the door," said Walter. "That's your crime. All I'm doing is walking through a door someone else opened."

"Yes... but why?" Minnie added.

"Because it's behind the scenes at a museum," Walter pointed out. *"Behind the scenes... at a museum!*

They'll have all the cool stuff back here. Delicate manuscripts, not in display cases. Fragile tunics, not in display cases."

Dennis, Minnie and Gnasher looked blankly at Walter.

"A tunic is a sort of shirt, but extra long," Walter informed them.

Dennis, Minnie and Gnasher looked blankly at Walter some more.

Minnie and Dennis were hugely disappointed with what faced them behind the door. The corridor was every bit as ordinary as the door itself. It was well lit, with the same strip lights they had at school. The brownish-yellowish tiled floor was clean. The pale-green walls could maybe do with a fresh coat of paint, like all corridors.

"This is **amazing!**" Walter exclaimed. "While the building itself dates back to Victorian times, it looks like, behind the scenes, the rooms and corridors were renovated in the 1970s."

Dennis rolled his eyes again. So hard that this time they almost rolled out of his head, rolled out of the museum, rolled home, rolled up the stairs and rolled into bed.

There were three doors in the corridor. The door they'd just come through, a door at the far end and a door halfway down. The door halfway had a window in it. The children peered in and saw a woman in a lab coat waving a hairdryer at a large block of ice.

"They're thawing something out!" Walter exclaimed, barging in.

"**Hey!** You can't come in here," the technician shouted as Minnie, Dennis and Gnasher followed.

"What are you thawing out?" Walter asked. "Is it a Castoroides?" He turned back to Minnie and Dennis. "Castoroides was a giant beaver. They grew to be bigger than a man."

"Never heard of 'em," Minnie said. "A beaver the size of a man should be called a Justin Beaver. Easier than Castoroides."

"**Get out!**" the technician shouted. "I don't know what it is until I thaw it out, now do I?"

Dennis stared at the ice block. There was something inside it, but exactly what, it was impossible to tell. The dark shape inside gave him a weird feeling.

The technician shooed them all out. "Go on, shoo!" she told them, and ushered them back out into the corridor.

Walter had a huge, annoying smile on his face. Saying that, any smile on Walter's face was in

some way annoying but this one seemed all the more annoying than usual.

Suddenly, the door at the end of the corridor flew open and a blinding light shone out. A powerful wind whirled around the group and they were all dragged along the corridor, then through the third and final door, which slammed shut behind them.

BUT WHAT ABOUT A BAD GUY?

I know what you're thinking. What about a bad guy? This is meant to be an awesome story, yeah? We're a bunch of pages in already, so where is he?

Well, the bad guy is here.

And by 'here', I mean upstairs in his office in the town hall. Yep, the bad guy is the Mayor.

And the Mayor was happy.

Happy because he had the Golden Yawning Penguin of Boringness!

Years ago, Gran had fired it into the sea. Or at least thought she had. She actually only shot it over the horizon, where it landed on a boat. Or rather, smashed into the deck of a boat. A cargo ship. The ship didn't sink, obviously, because that wouldn't be boring. Instead, the cargo ship went off on its journey and delivered its cargo to far-off lands.

In those far-off lands the Penguin was sold to a private collector of mysterious yet deadly boring items. That collector sold it on, then years later, it was sold to a museum in Yawntopia.

Never heard of Yawntopia? It's the world's most boring country. It was also mentioned a few chapters back, which just goes to show how boring it is if you've forgotten that already!

The head of antiquities at the Yawntopia National Museum heard that the long-lost Golden Yawning Penguin of Boringness was for sale and bought it for the museum. He thought it sounded a rather fitting exhibition piece.

And there it sat for decades to come. The most boring thing in the world, in the most boring country in the world.

Then, a couple of years ago, Beanotown got a new mayor. Wilbur Winston Brown. Wilbur hadn't always wanted to be mayor. At first (when he was four), he'd wanted to rule the world. Later (at ten), he'd realised that wasn't possible, so he set his sights on becoming prime minister.

But that was never to be. He failed.

But he did become Mayor of Beanotown, through hard work, determination and... printing all his own voting cards and owning the company that counted the votes.

His victory was short-lived, however.

While the Mayor was technically in charge of the town, he wasn't actually. No one was. The place itself was too unruly. No one was in charge of anything! Police and teachers tried their best, but it was impossible. Something was always escaping, falling over, breaking or generally misbehaving in the most mischievous and interesting ways.

If Wilbur was going to rule Beanotown with an iron fist, he'd have to make things a lot less interesting first.

So he had searched the net for boring places, for the most boring place on Earth...

THE CHAMBER OF MISCHIEF!

The children and Gnasher, having been dragged through the door by the mysterious wind, found themselves inside the Chamber of Mischief!

Actually, the wind had dragged them through the door and to a lift. The wind then pressed the button and everyone waited. Which was a bit awkward. When the lift came, the wind dragged them all inside. Then the wind waited again, and again things felt a bit weird.

"Would this not be a bit more dramatic if we'd been pulled down a dark, damp tunnel by a slimy tentacle or something?" Dennis asked the wind.

The wind didn't answer... because it was just the wind.

The wind waited a bit longer, then an annoyed voice came over the tannoy.

"Press the button!" the voice said. "You need to press the button or it won't go anywhere."

The wind felt a bit silly and pressed the down button. The doors closed and the lift went down.

Then they were in the Chamber of Mischief.

Dennis, Gnasher, Minnie and Walter looked around at the small cave, which had various tunnels leading off from it (the wind disappeared back up in the lift).

In front of them, sat on a large chair, was a duck. A small china duck.

"I am the Guardian of the Pea-shooter," it said, in the same voice that they'd heard in the lift.

"You're a duck," said Dennis.

"I may be a duck," shouted the duck, "but mainly I'm the Guardian of the Pea-shooter. Do you dare face the challenges of the chamber, to see if you're worthy of wielding the Golden Pea-shooter?"

Minnie frowned. "McGlinchy sent us down here. He wants us to have the thing. So hand it over!"

"It's me McGlinchy wants to have the Pea-shooter," Dennis interjected. "So hand it over!"

"I am Lord Duckinson," the duck announced. "I am the Guardian of the Pea – "

"You're a little china duck that somehow ended up alive in a museum and was sent down here to make sure losers don't get the Pea-shooter. But we're not losers. We're far from it, so hand it over!" Dennis interrupted.

"I'm the Guardian! *I* say who gets the Pea-shooter!" the tiny duck shouted.

"Alright, then," said Dennis. "How much do you want for it? You can put it on my bill."

"Buy it? You can't do that! **Where do you think you are?** You have to do the challenges to prove you're worthy!"

"McGlinchy did say things had got out of control," Minnie muttered.

"Alright!" Dennis shouted. "We'll complete the challenges. Where's the first one?"

And, just like that, a giant tentacle slid into view and dragged the four of them sideways, down a dark, damp tunnel.

DUN! DUN! DUUUN! MATHS!

Dennis, Minnie, Gnasher and Walter were now in a huge cavern. The floor in front of them was covered in coloured hexagonal tiles each the size of a shield. Each tile had a number from one to twelve carved into it and beyond the tiles was a large door. Oh, and the giant octopus who'd just yoinked them here was sat in the middle of the floor, barring their way with a very menacing look upon his face.

"Welcome..." the giant octopus boomed, "to the first challenge in the Chamber of Mischief! I am Addiron, and I challenge you to a game of skill and luck."

Walter started to walk across the tiles and the octopus slapped him with a huge, wet tentacle. SPLATCH!

Minnie, Dennis and Gnasher laughed.

"Calamari," Walter said through gritted teeth and quietly swore revenge in his head.

"No cheating!" the octopus ordered. "You have to play to get across! That's the only way to the next challenge."

"Fine!" said Dennis. "How do we do it?"

The enormous octopus rubbed two of his tentacles together.

"Excellent! This game requires two dice."

"I've got a dice app on my phone," Dennis said, pulling his phone out of his pocket.

Pulling his phone out of his pocket was something Dennis rarely did. His phone was embarrassing, as it was his mum's old phone before she got a proper one. It was made by a company that no one had heard of and was thicker than toast. He didn't really want it, but his mum made him carry it. "For emergencies," she'd insisted and loaded it with the minimum amount of credit to prevent him making prank calls.

"There's a bunch of free dice apps in the app store. I got one of them."

"Has anyone ever told you, you can be really annoying at times?" Addiron asked Dennis.

"All the time!" Walter answered for him.

"Start in any grey zone. Having rolled, you must move, unless it's impossible. Try to make the next number in front of you from the numbers on your dice. You can either by add, subtract, divide or multiply the numbers you have rolled."

Dennis rolled and got a 5 and a 1, which he easily turned into a 4, and he was off.

I can do this! Dennis thought. *I can win!*

Make your way across the board. If you are forced onto a space with a banana skin, then start again.

He stood a really good chance and anyway, there were three kids playing against one octopus, so only one of them had to win. The odds were four to one in their favour.

Addiron won, but only because he was really good at Maths.

"Ha! Ha! Ha! **I won!**" he shouted. "Go on then, off you go. Through to the next chamber."

The children looked at each other, puzzled.

"You're letting us through to the next chamber?" Minnie asked in disbelief.

"Yeah, sure! It's just through that little door there," the octopus said with a smile.

"But we lost," Dennis pointed out.

"I don't think that matters. You just have to play the game," Addiron replied.

The children shrugged and walked through to the next chamber.

Then Addiron thought *have I got that right?* and rang the Guardian's office to double-check.

"Hi, Mr Lord Duckinson... I just want to double-check. Once people complete the task, let them through, yeah...? Okay. Good. Just wanted to make sure."

The enormous octopus thought again.

"Does 'complete' mean win or just finish...? Oh, it means win? Right, well, you really should have been less woolly in your language..."

The octopus squinted as Lord Duckinson's angry quacks came from the other end of the phone.

I STUDIED IN VENICE!

The next room was a much smaller room, filled with easels. All the easels surrounded a table in the middle of the room, which groaned under the weight of the enormous fruit. The banana was as big as a dad and the other fruit matched that size. An old-fashioned painting hung on the far wall. A self-portrait of an old, long dead master.

"This is art, isn't it?!" Dennis exclaimed. "All these challenges are school-based. That's what McGlinchy meant when he said it's not the sort of thing kids are into... **Urrrgh!**"

"Come in! Come in!" beckoned the figure in the painting. "Take an easel, any easel. We're very casual here."

The children looked at each other with puzzled looks, as though they'd never seen a living, talking painting before. Dennis shrugged. He quite liked art. Going to school on a day on which they had art was a bit easier than other days.

"What do we have to do here?" Walter asked. "What's the challenge?"

"Paint the fruit," the painting said.

"And how do you win?" Minnie asked.

The painting looked offended.

"This is art!" it said. "You can't win or lose in Art. It's about self-expression."

The children looked at the painting blankly. Gnasher did that thing dogs do and tilted his head.

A phone started ringing.

"Wait, sorry. I'm getting a call," the painting said, and the 2D picture answered its 2D phone. "Hello? Oh, hello Lord Duckinson. I was just explaining to the children here that there's no way to win or lose at art. That it's..." The painting stopped to listen to Lord Duckinson's angry quacks. "What do you mean 'find a way to have losers?' This is art! I was telling the children that creating a piece of art is a unique problem. A problem that hasn't existed

The living portrait wants to express himself. Can you complete the painting's reflection in the mirror?

before and–" The 300-year-old painting stopped as Lord Duckinson interrupted again.

"That's offensive!" the painting shouted down the phone. "A spot-the-difference competition? I studied in **Venice!**"

The painting hung up.

"Go through, children!" it cried to the kids. "Go on! Next challenge. Go on. I can't paint in this mood."

The children walked through to the next challenge. So far, things had been pretty easy. They were about to get a lot harder.

YOU BIG, STINKY
FUZZBALL!

The group found themselves in a long corridor. The high ceiling was held up with stone pillars. Leaning against the walls were every sort of weapon and armour imaginable.

"I like this room," said Minnie, nodding appreciatively.

"This looks suspiciously like a history challenge," Dennis said.

In the middle of the corridor, barring their way, was an enormous knight in black armour. Weirdly, he looked much more frightening than the giant octopus. He stood easily 8-feet tall and his head almost touched the ceiling. Then, from his helmet came a terrible voice.

"Whomsoever..."

A phone started ringing.

The knight held up its hand to the kids, huffed

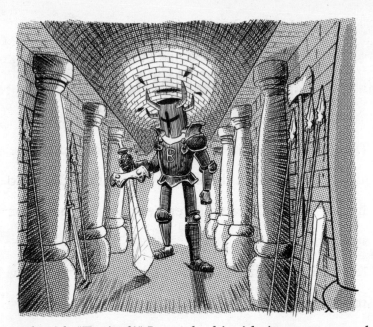

and said, "Typical!" It reached inside its armour and pulled out a small phone. "I'm busy, can this wait...? Yeah, they're here now. I was just going to... yes, of course there'll be winners and losers. No, what sort of idiot would let losers through...? Well, what do you expect when you put a squid and a painting in charge?"

There was furious quacking from the other end of the line.

"You want me to kill the losers, yeah?" asked the knight.

The kids all gasped and stepped back. "Okay, fine, I promise not to harm any of them."

He hung up, looking seriously narked.

"Phew!" the children all phewed.

"Okay," said the knight, "I was thinking we'd have an epic battle to the death, but Lord Duckinson says we don't have the licence for that," he sighed. "So instead you'll have to figure out what the runes are saying."

The knight pointed to the wall beside them and strange writing started to appear on it, carved into the wall.

"Cool powers, man – I'm glad we don't have to battle you!" said Dennis.

The knight was angrily grinding his teeth.

"What've we gotta do here?" Dennis asked. "Figure out what the secret word is? I bet it's 'password' – "

"It's not 'password'," the dark knight muttered, glaring at him.

"All the passwords on my parents' computers are 'password'-"

"It's not 'password'!"

The knight had clearly lost his temper. He pointed at Dennis, sending out a bolt of purple lightning from his finger, which zapped the boy... who instantly disappeared.

Minnie, Walter and Gnasher looked, wide-eyed, at the space where Dennis, er, wasn't.

"Where'd he go?" Minnie asked.

"This is the history challenge, so now he's in it!" the knight said. "About 500 years ago. You'll never see him again."

"Yes!" Walter exclaimed, punching the air. "Ha! Ha! Ha!"

***

The knight was rubbish at sending people back in time, but had no idea because no one had ever made it back to tell him. Dennis didn't appear 500 years ago. Instead, he appeared 22,000 years ago.

Dennis appeared in an ice age, in his shorts.

The ice age had started a bit more than two million years ago and was nearing the end. It only had about a thousand years left. But that really wasn't much use to Dennis. The wind blew colder than Dennis had ever felt in his life. Snow blasted into his face. It seemed like it was daytime, but it was getting darker. The snow was blocking out the sun.

I need a big woolly coat, like that mammoth! Dennis thought, because he was too cold to speak. Then, as the mammoth ran towards him, he thought: *I need to get away from that mammoth!*

Dennis tried to run, but the snow was too deep. He sunk below the surface and had to lift his feet up as high as he could to get them onto the next patch of snow. With each step, the snow would give way and his foot would sink in again. Later, when Dennis described this bit to me, he said his progress was 'massively slow'.

As the mammoth raced towards him, Dennis was suddenly lit by a spotlight from above. It was from a small spaceship that flew down and landed a little way in front of him.

What is a spaceship doing here? thought Dennis. *What are the chances?*

But a glance over his shoulder revealed that the angry mammoth was terrifyingly close. He dived under the snow. The ground around him shook as the mammoth charged past, centimetres from Dennis. He wanted to stay under the snow for longer, until it was definitely safe, but he couldn't bear the horrendous cold for more than a few seconds.

He came up, just as the mammoth's mammoth bottom disappeared into the thickening snowstorm.

"Go on, **you big, stinky fuzzball!** Get lost!" Dennis shouted after it as the hairy beast trampled over the small spacecraft.

A moment later, the mammoth couldn't be seen any more. Peering through the growing blizzard,

Dennis spotted a small, cat-sized alien staggering out of the now dented ship. Dennis had quite a few questions for the strange creature, like 'Wha?' and 'Huh?' and 'Eh?'

The creature looked cross. It looked crossly at Dennis, as if it were blaming him somehow. Then it started to type into a device mounted on its wrist and – ZIIIP! – it disappeared. Dennis couldn't believe his eyes.

The snow blew harder. Dennis couldn't see anything now. No cave. No trees or bushes or any cover at all. The wind blew harder and the snow fell heavier. He knew that if he couldn't find a way of

surviving the next five minutes, getting back to his own time would be impossible.

"Stupid snow!" he shouted at the sky. "Where's snow like this on school days?"

Dennis felt sleepy for some reason, even though every bit of him hurt. He collapsed into the snow. His red-and-black jumper was only visible for a few seconds, before the snow covered him completely...

Then he screamed and fell out of an ice block.

"Arrrgh! That is well cold!" he shouted, shaking and kicking ice off himself.

The technician, who had just thawed Dennis out with the hairdryer, stumbled back.

"But, but... but you were only in here ten minutes ago!" she protested.

Dennis ran over to the radiator, which was thankfully on, and hugged it.

"W-W-what just h-happened?" he asked, looking around.

He was in the lab or whatever it was where the technician lady had been thawing out the thing in the ice.

Dennis looked back at the now much-reduced ice block. The thing in the ice had gone.

"That ice is thousands of years old," the technician pointed out. "How did you get in it?"

"**Whoa!** Hold on! I was in the ice?!" Dennis exclaimed, while fiddling with the thermostat on the side of the radiator. "Earlier, when I-I-I was looking in the ice, I-I-I was looking at myself!?! M-m-makes s-s-sense, I g-guess."

"No it doesn't!" said the technician. She seemed to be offended by how little sense the situation made.

"P-P-point that hairdryer at me!" Dennis demanded. "I'm still f-f-freezing!"

Still shivering, three minutes later Dennis stepped out of the lift into the Chamber of Mischief. Again. Lord Duckinson fixed him with a steely stare.

"Didn't you...?"

"Yeah, I did," Dennis replied, and barged through into maths.

As he walked in, Addiron, the octopus, gave him a puzzled look.

"Didn't you just...?" and he pointed to the door to art, with a tentacle.

"D-dude! I don't want to t-talk about it!" Dennis answered as he walked briskly across the game to the next door, hugging himself.

Dennis got a similar look off the painting in the art challenge.

"Didn't you just...?" the painting started to say, but Dennis held his hand up to shush him.

"Not now!"

Dennis burst into history just seconds after the dark knight had made him disappear, and even the helmet of the dark knight looked shocked.

"We must be getting near Cringebeard's Golden P-Pea-shooter of Everlasting F-Fun, because the Golden Yawning Penguin of Boringness doesn't seem to be having any effect in here."

***

Let's just pause for a moment to admire that last thing Dennis said. I'm pretty sure that's the first time those words have ever been said in that order.

***

"How did you escape the past?" asked the shocked knight.

"I built a time machine out of bones and sticks," Dennis lied. "Now, where were we?"

"We have to figure out what this says," Walter

reminded him, pointing at some strange markings on the wall. "Using the key."

"I'll leave that to you, Walts," Dennis said. "I'd rather not go through what I just went through again."

"'Walts'?" said Walter, disgusted at his new name.

Minnie turned sweetly to him with a smile. "Just get on with it, Walts!"

And you know what? Walter figured it out.

ABCDEFG

HIJKLMN

OPQRSTU

VWXYZ

What does this say?

Can you solve the code?

_____

EINGLISH!

I spelt English wrong in the chapter title here, just to annoy my old English teacher. Look, Mr Grim! They've let me write a book for kids and it's got the word 'English' spelt wrong in it! Ha! Ha! Ha!

'Spelt wrong' is probably wrong, too. It should be something like 'incorrectly spelt' or something.

Spelt wrong! Spelt wrong! Ha! Ha! Ha!

Where was I...? Oh yeah...

* * *

The children walked down a long, thin corridor to the next challenge. It was so narrow they had to walk in single file. Dennis, Minnie and Gnasher walked behind Walter. They were still suspicious of him, but he had just got them through the history challenge. Maybe he wasn't that bad... okay, he was still annoying and his voice had that tone that made you instantly think *I wish this guy would shut up*, but he was sort of bearable. Just.

The next room was roughly classroom-size. Which was good really, as it was a classroom.

"Urrrgh!" Minnie and Dennis groaned.

Their groan seemed to wake up a pile of dusty old bones in the seat behind the teacher's desk. They were moving and fitting together to form a skeleton.

"Muuurgh," it groaned as it rose.

"Arrrgh!" shouted the children as they made a dash for the door they'd come in through. Unfortunately, that was now locked.

Gnasher's reaction to the zombie teacher was different. He ran over to her and stole her leg bone.

"Hey!" shouted the undead educator. "I need that!"

It was then the children got a proper look at the frightening faculty member. She was a zombie alright, and not one of the fresh ones. She was mostly just skeleton, though there was enough skin left on her face to tell that she was angry.

"Whose dog is this?" she questioned. "No dogs in class!"

"Hey now, technically, he's sort of my dog, in a way," Dennis tried to explain. "But he's very much a free agent. I'm not like his boss or anything."

"Just simmer down! All of you. Find a seat," the decomposing disciplinarian said. "This challenge is English."

Dennis groaned. It was his least favourite of all the subjects.

"This is a test for all three of you. First

question. What does 'malodorous' mean? Is it–"

"It means stinky, miss!" Minnie said, putting her hand up.

"Let me finish!" said the teacher. "Is it evil...?"

"No! It means **stinky**, miss," Minnie shouted.

"Fish-like or–"

"Stinky, miss," Minnie interrupted.

"Or stinky?" the zombie teacher glowered at Minnie (which means scowl or glare). "Next question! What does 'disputatious' mean? Is it–"

"It means you like having an argument, miss," Minnie interrupted.

"Wait till I've finished the question!" the zombie teacher demanded.

"I'm disputatious because I like a good row!" Minnie told the teacher. "I'm a most disputatious girl," she said proudly.

"Monticule?"

"A really small mountain!" Minnie beamed.

"Deciduous?"

"Trees and that what drop their leaves in autumn," Minnie said, with her best smug face.

"Arrrgh!" the teacher screamed. "You've got one of those 'word of the day' calendars in your house, haven't you?"

"Yes," replied Minnie. "My progenitor (parent) thought it would be a good idea."

"Okay," said Dennis. "Can we go now? This was stupid, anyway. Nothing like a proper chamber. 'cept maybe the Chamber of Lame!"

"Grrrah!" the zombie teacher growled and stood to her full height (on one leg because Gnasher was nomming on the other). Then the bones she was made of dropped out of the air and fell in a pile on the floor.

"Great, we've completed another challenge," cried Minnie.

"Erm, I'm not sure about that.." replied Walter.

Suddenly, the powerful wind that had pulled them into the chamber via the lift appeared. It picked up the tables and chairs, and flew them around the children's heads. Then it ripped the ceiling off the classroom to reveal a cave roof, high above. The walls crumbled away as did the narrow corridor, collapsing into the bottomless void surrounding them. The edges of the classroom floor were next to go, falling into the yawning black pit below.

Dennis began to wonder whether Beanotown suffered from a bit of a wind problem, perhaps from

the exessive use of whoopee cushions. It seemed like a small price to pay.

"Chamber of Lame?" Minnie asked Dennis, sarcastically.

"**Hey!** You annoyed her loads more than me!" Dennis snapped back.

"Let's agree you're **both** to blame!" Walter shouted over the roar of the wind. "Now, what do we do to survive this?"

Suddenly the wind stopped, the tables

and chairs in the air dropped down into the pit below, and the classroom floor stopped growing smaller.

The cavern was huge. The remaining patch of 'floor' they were standing on didn't seem to be held up by anything.

"That's the door to the next challenge," said Dennis, spotting it in the wall on the far side of the cavern.

"How are we meant to get to that?" Walter asked.

Gnasher looked up from the bone of his teacher for a moment, then went back to chewing it.

Large slabs of stone rose up out of the darkness, each with a random word on it. The slabs floated around, moving all the time.

"Here are some words you know," said the voice of the teacher. "Some are linked, some are not. Jump on the connected words in the right order to get across. The first word is, 'dinner'".

They all jumped across to 'dinner'.

"What's the second word, then?" Dennis asked.

Gnasher thought he knew and jumped over to the stone with 'sausage' carved into it.

Which fell like the stone it was.

"Gnasher! No!" shouted Dennis as he saw him plunge into the darkness. A tear came to Dennis's eye. "Dumb dog. He thinks 'sausage' is the right answer to every question!"

"What's next?" asked Minnie. "It's got to be 'dinner table'," she called and jumped across.

The slab held for her, Dennis and, lastly, Walter.

"So the next one's gotta be 'potato'," said Walter. "You know, because of the 'table potato'."

"'Table potato'?" asked Dennis.

"Yeah. It's like a potato," said Walter. "Really big and flat. They make great mash."

"Whatever," said Minnie, and she and Dennis jumped over to the 'potato' stone.

Can you figure out the word chain to make your way across the abyss?

dinner-table-top-dog-biscuit-tin

133

It shifted beneath their feet then plummeted down into the abyss.

"Ha! Ha! Ha! **I lied!**" Walter shouted down as they fell. "Oh! and did I mention that I'm here for the Pea-shooter myself, and it was no accident that I was there near the entrance to the Chamber of Mischief when you found me? This is a double-cross!"

Actually, because Dennis was falling, Walter got quieter and quieter as the distance between them grew, so Walter sounded like this:

"Ha! Ha! Ha! I lied! Oh! and did I mention that I'm here for the Pea-shooter myself, and it was no accident that I was there near the entrance to the Chamber of Mischief when you found me? This is a double-cross!"

Dennis and Minnie fell into blackness.

"That's it, Minnie!" Dennis said. "Beanotown is doomed! If Walter gets the Pea-shooter, his will be the only tricks that work. He'll take over in no time."

* * *

Back in the town hall, the Mayor chuckled to himself. *Soon*, he thought. *Soon my son will have the Golden Pea-shooter. And I can* **destroy it!** *Beanotown will be like any other normal town, without any comical catastrophes, skateboarding pensioners or menacing children. At last, I will rule Beanotown... with an iron fist!*

HOW LONG IS ETERNITY?

Meanwhile, Dennis was getting bored of falling.

He looked below him and saw a distant light growing. A few minutes later, Dennis and Minnie landed with a bump.

He didn't recognise it as detention to begin with. The first thing he became aware of was that he'd landed perfectly on one of the chairs that had fallen down there earlier. All the classroom tables and chairs were there, unbroken and neatly arranged.

Minnie was sitting next to him, leaning back on her chair, balancing a pen on her top lip. Gnasher was sitting the other side of him with a surprised expression on his face.

"Gnasher!" Dennis shouted. "You're alright!" He threw his arms around him.

"Simmer... down," said the giant talking tortoise at the front of the class.

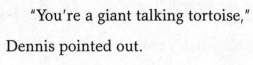

"You're a giant talking tortoise," Dennis pointed out.

"Yes... I... know," the tortoise said slowly.

"It knows," said Minnie, and went back to balancing her pen.

"I find it hard to believe McGlinchy built all this," Dennis said. "He couldn't do magic when Gran knew him and he's just an old dude now, he couldn't have put all this together."

"Oh no... he didn't," the tortoise slowly told Dennis.

"He didn't," Minnie told Dennis.

"Mr McGlinchy just... put the Golden... Pea-shooter... down here... to keep it... safe. Then... whenever a mysterious item... with magical powers... came to the museum... put it... down here, too... To guard it."

"You're a tortoise," Dennis pointed out again. "They don't put tortoises in museums."

"I'm actually a... living... stone... statue... of a tortoise," the tortoise slowly pointed out.

Now that the tortoise said it, it was obvious that it was a statue. It had a very stony look and on its back was a carving of a castle with a tall tower growing out of the centre.

"It's a living stone statue of a tortoise," Minnie told Dennis.

"How'd the giant octopus get here, then?" asked Dennis. "That's obviously not a statue."

"There's a giant... octopus... down here now... is there?" the tortoise asked slowly.

"Yes!"

"Well... that doesn't make any sense," the living statue slowly complained. "This is a museum... not... an aquarium."

"We're getting off track!" Dennis said. "We need to figure out how to escape this place."

"There is... no... escape," the tortoise said slowly.

"There is no escape," Minnie repeated.

"This is... detention!" the statue told Dennis.

It was then that Dennis realised he was in detention.

"Detention?!" Dennis exclaimed. "For how long?"

"Eternity."

"What? Like all day?"

"No... eternity... means... forever."

"So a week, then?"

"Longer than... a week. It's... eternity."

"But I'll be out by my birthday, right?"

"You'll... never... be out. This detention will last... forever," the tortoise statue slowly told Dennis.

"That sounds well boring. How did this happen?" Dennis demanded to know.

"Me," said the stone tortoise, slowly. "While you're near me... you will age as quickly as a stone tortoise. Which is... not at all. Time doesn't really move... forwards... here, look."

The tortoise slowly pointed to an empty patch of cave wall and a clock suddenly appeared. The second hand on the clock wasn't moving.

"Urrrrrgh!" Dennis groaned.

"Now you're on the same page as me," Minnie told Dennis.

"Look on... the bright side," said the statue, slowly. "Over the next... few hundred... thousand... years... you'll be able to catch up on... your homework."

"Can't," said Dennis. "No books."

"Oh... you can have books... if you want," said the tortoise, and around them stacks of hundreds of books appeared. Then stacks of hundreds more appeared on those stacks. Then about twelve more books, in a disappointing final blip.

One glance at these told Dennis what he needed to know. School books. Nothing awesome.

No adventures. A lot of it was stuff about the Middle Ages.

It took a couple of days for Minnie and Dennis to realise they didn't need to eat or go to the toilet or sleep in detention.

While Dennis built a stack of books up to the clock so he could push the hands round himself, he thought about what must be going on high above them.

Walter must have got the Golden Pea-shooter by now and must be ruling Beanotown with an iron fist, or something.

Dennis thought this because he didn't understand what was really going on. Days, weeks, years in detention were only detention days, weeks and years. Outside, time was passing at a different rate.

If you've ever spent time in detention yourself, you'll know that it felt like a week, but when you left it was only half an hour later.

Have you ever had to go to a wedding? They're the same. That thing in the church you had to sit through was only an hour long. That's like half the length of a cool movie, but it felt like sitting through ten lame movies, didn't it?

The hands on the clock wouldn't move. Upon close inspection, it turned out they were drawn on. Dennis sat back down for a week or so.

The stone tortoise teacher didn't act like a teacher. It let the children do whatever they wanted and didn't mind them talking. Dennis found a straw and fired a bunch of paper pellets at the tortoise, but the tortoise didn't shout at Dennis. All it did was stare at, and slow down, the pellets as they travelled through the air, until they actually stopped in mid-air. The tortoise would then slowly walk out of the way and then allow the paper balls to fly into the wall.

"That's annoying!" Dennis told the tortoise.

The tortoise just smiled.

A day or so later, as the tortoise slowly walked past Dennis, Dennis gave the castle on its back a closer look. Through the tiny window in the top of the tiny tower, Dennis saw that there was a tiny princess combing her hair. The princess saw Dennis watching her and looked cross.

This has got absolutely nothing to do with any of the rest of the story, but it did happen.

"Urrrgh!" Dennis shouted. "How is this not over yet?"

The tortoise frowned at Dennis. It had explained the eternity thing already. Was it really going to have to explain eternity, for eternity?

"There must be a way out of here," Dennis said, looking around at the walls he'd looked at thousands of times before.

Then a huge, old leather book landed on the desk in front of him with a crash.

"Did you do that?" Dennis asked the tortoise. "I told you, I'm not reading any boring school books about oxbow lakes or whatever."

"Wasn't me," the stone tortoise told Dennis.

Dennis opened it and read the title: *The Book of Everything.*

On the second page... there was nothing.

Dennis sat in a different chair for eight days. Just to mix things up. Minnie sat where Dennis had been sitting. She opened *The Book of Everything* and stared at the second page for a while before turning her head to look at the third page. She laughed. Then laughed again.

"What are you laughing at **nothing** for?" Dennis shouted over to Minnie.

"It's funny!" Minnie shouted back.

"There's nothing in it," Dennis said, throwing his hands up.

"No, there is. It's got a funny story in it. It's called 'The Fart that Turned Everyone into Zombies'. It's about this girl who does a pump so bad it turns everyone into zombies, so she has to hide out at the museum where all the awesome retro weapons are. It's like an action comedy!"

Dennis leapt up and ran over. "What a load of..." But, before he could say 'pants', he saw that the book was indeed full of words.

"What's the deal here?" Dennis asked the stone tortoise. "When I first looked in this thing it had nothing in it."

"I don't... know," answered the tortoise, really slowly, walking over, slowly. It looked at the book (slowly). It read for a few moments, then (slowly) said, "This isn't a story about a bottom burp that... turns people into... the undead. It's a story about... a lonely tortoise's search for... love."

Minnie grabbed the book and scanned the pages. "No it's not! This is all about fighting guff zombies with Viking weapons."

"It's another magic museum thingy! Remember? It was up in the museum, in with all that other weird junk. Between the steam-powered robot and the thingy of whatever," Dennis told them. "It's whatever you want it to be. You want a funny story

about zombies. It's that. You want a story about a tortoise in search of romance? It's that!"

"I am... currently... looking... for love," the tortoise slowly admitted.

"How come it was empty for you, then?" asked Minnie.

"**Urrrgh!** Because I didn't want to read. Because I thought it was going to be a boring school book."

Dennis grabbed the book, shut it and held it to his chest, screwing his eyes up tight.

"Come on! Come " he said to himself, slamming the book down on the desk and opening it at page two.

'How to Escape Detention' was the new title.

TINY

Having escaped detention in the most amazing, fantastic, dangerous, funny, exciting, entertaining way possible, Dennis, Minnie, Gnasher and the detention tortoise found themselves in the next Chamber of Mischief.

I can't stress how amazing and fantastic, and all those other words, the escape from detention was. It's a bit odd that I haven't put it in this book. It would have been the best bit. So I'm saving it for the next one. Got to keep my publisher happy and all that...

***

"I'll see you later," the tortoise said quickly. "And thanks for everything." Then he whooshed off at incredible speed, to go on a hot date he'd read about.

The trio looked at the scene before them. They were in a huge cave. The biggest yet. It formed an enormous dome you could fit a mountain in. A really small mountain (a monticule, in fact, as we learnt earlier in English), but still a mountain.

The space didn't have a mountain in it, though. Floating in mid-air was a beach ball-sized glowing yellow ball and under it, carpeting the ground, was a town.

A small town. Not a town made of very few buildings but a town made of a lot of buildings that was small. A large tiny town.

Minnie looked down. She saw that the puddle they were standing in had tiny waves and tiny boats. From this high up she could see the water even had a tiny whale in it. She looked at the tiny beach, 30 centimetres in front of them, and saw a tiny red-and-black-striped lighthouse.

"This must be geography," said Dennis. "Because it's some, er, geography. Though I don't see any oxbow lakes."

"That looks like Beanotown lighthouse!" Minnie exclaimed.

Dennis looked closer. "This is Beanotown!" he said. "Look! There's the school. There's the top-secret research station. The haunted library. There's Mount Beano. The museum. It's all here!"

"Everyone's here, too!" Minnie said, pointing at the tiny people on the beach running away screaming in terror.

Dennis stepped out of the sea and very carefully stepped onto land, utterly destroying a house near the shore as he did so.

"I hope they weren't in!" said Dennis.

Looking down, he saw that a tiny old lady carrying two shopping bags was jumping up and down, shouting angrily at him. She was too small for him to hear, but it looked like she was swearing.

"Sorry!" said Dennis, but it didn't seem to do much good.

"Careful what you're doing, you big idiot!" warned Minnie, accidentally crushing an ice-cream van near the beach.

The tiny ice-cream man, who'd only just managed to jump free in time, ran to safety.

"Let's none of us move until we figure out what we've actually got to do," suggested Dennis.

Gnasher saw some tiny humans hiding under the jetty by the beach. He sniffed at them and one of them got sucked up into his nose.

Gnasher shook his head and sneezed Bernard (for that was his name) out onto the beach, covered in dog snot. It was the worst thing that had ever happened to him. To Bernard, that is. Gnasher always enjoyed a good snotty sneeze.

Further inland, Tiny Dennis looked up and saw the enormous Dennis towering above the tiny town.

"Hey, look! Mum! **It's me!**" he shouted to his mum.

Tiny Dennis's mum looked up at the huge Godzilla-sized Dennis and, knowing what her beloved son was like, she said, **"We're doomed!"**

The model town had been built in the back garden of the only pub in (normal-sized) Beanotown, The Alarmed Llama, as a tourist attraction 100 years ago. It had worked at first. Everyone in the town had come to see the model and marvel at the great detail Algernon, the pub owner, had put into it. There were even tiny model people of the townsfolk.

There was a slight pick-up in tourists after lightning struck the model Beanotown and all the tiny model people were brought to life (because anything struck by lightning in Beanotown comes to life).

And now, as the people of Beanotown grew older, so did the model people. When a baby was born in Beanotown, a tiny baby was born in tiny Beanotown. Life in the tiny town mirrored life in the big town.

People came to see if they could spot themselves, but those who did saw that the tiny version of themselves was usually screaming in terror, and that wasn't much fun. Over time, the novelty simply wore off. Bad vibes are bad vibes, after all.

Eventually, Algernon managed to sell it to the museum as 'an important artefact of local history'.

Tiny Dennis jumped on his skateboard and whizzed down to the seafront, to try to meet his larger self. His tiny mum tried to stop him, but he was too fast. His tiny dog, Gnasher, followed.

It was only when he started getting closer that Tiny Dennis realised how enormous the outsider Dennis was. His head was as high as the sun!

Tiny Dennis made it to Normal-sized Dennis's shoe. The shoe that was in the wreckage of the old lady's house. Luckily Normal-sized Dennis hadn't done his laces up properly, so Tiny Dennis was able to climb the lace to the top of the shoe. He looked up at the climb ahead of him and his tiny head spun.

"Gnasher! **Get up here!**" he shouted to Tiny Gnasher.

Normal-sized Gnasher, with his excellent hearing, heard his name but couldn't quite tell where it had come from.

"Ow!" shouted Normal-sized Dennis, lifting his foot to grab his ankle. "I've been stung," he said.

Tiny Gnasher – who had just GNASHED Normal-sized Dennis on the ankle – jumped off just in time as Tiny Dennis held on to the lace. As Normal-sized Dennis rubbed the bite for a moment, Tiny Dennis leapt onto his larger self's sleeve. He held on to the wool, which to him was like the thick ropes used to tie ships to the dock.

Normal-sized Dennis put his foot back down and brought his hand up to his head to give it a scratch as he tried to figure out the geography challenge.

Tiny Dennis saw his chance and dropped down onto his larger self's ear. Then he slid down the outside until he got as far as the earhole. His original plan was to climb inside. But Normal-sized Dennis's ear was as clean as his, so he stayed at the entrance and shouted.

"Don't stick your finger in your ear or you'll squash me!"

"Whoa!" said Normal-sized Dennis at hearing his own voice in his ear. "My thoughts are talking to me!"

"I'm not your thoughts," said Tiny Dennis. "I'm the tiny you!"

"Minnie!" said Normal-sized Dennis. "Look in my ear."

Minnie did and, with a lot less surprise than you'd think, said, "Dude. There's a tiny you in your ear."

"Cool!" said Dennis. "How do we do this challenge?"

"It's easy," said the voice in his ear. "You've just got to find all the stuff listed on the map on the wall behind you, then you'll be teleported to the next chamber."

Dennis turned to look at the wall. There was a grid map of the town stuck onto the wall.

"Enormous Walter did it in two minutes," said Tiny Dennis.

"Enormous Walter?!" Dennis exclaimed. "How big is *he*?"

"He's **huge!**" Tiny Dennis told him. "As huge as you."

"Oh. Normal-sized," said Dennis, relaxing. "Where's the top-secret research station?"

"Seven squares east. Six squares north," Tiny Dennis informed him.

From the station, to find the library they then looked one square east and six squares south. From there, to find Dinosaur Island they looked three squares east and from there, to find the museum, they looked three squares north and eight squares west.

Tiny Dennis told Normal-sized Dennis to put his ear to the ground so he could jump to the floor.

"Later, dude!" he shouted.

"Do we get teleported now or something?" asked Dennis, and he, Minnie and Gnasher disappeared.

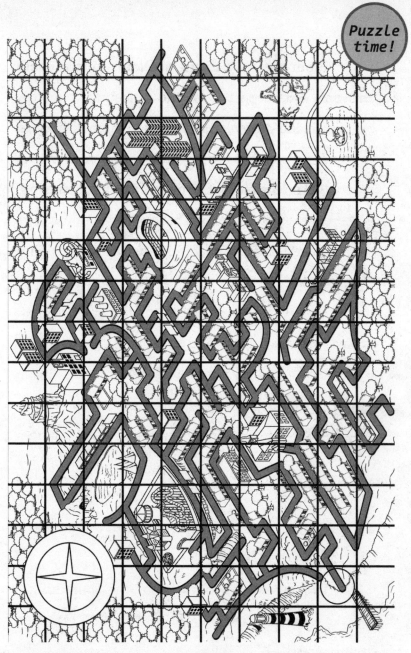

Start in the circle near the lighthouse and find the top-secret research centre, the library, Dinosaur Island and the museum.

From the tiny town hall (one square south and one square east from the museum), two tiny bespectacled eyes jealously watched them disappear.

If I were that big I'd have complete and total control over this town! the tiny Mayor thought.

YAWNTOPIA

Earlier I told you how the Mayor had searched for boring places, to find out how they achieved such boringness, so that he might make Beanotown just as dull.

Well, he soon found Yawntopia – the most boring place in the world. Using the town's school dinners fund, Wilbur booked a flight straight there.

Wilbur found Yawntopia delightful.

No one was smiling. No one seemed happy. No one was being unruly. **Zero** exciting things were happening. In fact there was nothing, anywhere, of any interest.

To understand it better, the Mayor decided to find out about the country's history, and what better place to do that than the museum.

It had been Wilbur's intention to spend some time wandering the museum. Finding out what he could about the region. He thought he would perhaps have to look at the museum records. Go back through countless newspapers. Carefully study the artefacts.

But just as you enter central Yawntopia's museum, the first artefact you see – the artefact that has pride of place in the entrance hall – is the Golden Yawning Penguin of Boringness! Under which was written:

The Golden Yawning Penguin of Boringness.

340 BC

Said to have magical powers of extreme boringness, this gold statue once belonged to a lost tribe of teachers from deepest Yawntopia. Lost for many years, it was returned to Yawntopia in 1982.

It seemed to call to him, in much the same way as the Pea-shooter had called to Katie and now Dennis. He knew, without knowing how, that this was the source of all Yawntopia's boringness.

(He was actually wrong about this. Yawntopia is a naturally boring place. For those of you who enjoy geography, the ground around Yawntopia has heavy deposits of yawntainium and there are natural underground springs of boringness. But the Penguin did add to it greatly.)

Wilbur grabbed the Penguin and ran.

Normally when such things happen in museums, alarms ring. Red lights flash and something goes AWOOOGA! Then lots of strong security guards run after you, then catch you and punch you until you let go of whatever you grabbed.

This sort of thing is exciting to see for those not getting hit by guards, and definitely not boring for the person getting bashed.

So that didn't happen.

What happened was: Wilbur picked it up... and the alarm failed to go off. As red lights didn't

flash, Wilbur ran out, and as the AWOOOGA-thing didn't go AWOOOGA!, Wilbur looked back to see guards weren't chasing him.

He slowed his run to a walk, as he felt a bit silly running from nothing, and went back to his hotel.

He had booked two weeks in Yawntopia, thinking it wouldn't be that easy to find Yawntopia's secret. But lots of investigating and looking for clues might have been interesting, so there was no chance of that in such a boring town.

Wilbur did nothing for the next two weeks except sit by the hotel pool. It was intensely boring.

He loved every minute of it.

THE GAME OF TOMORROW

Dennis, Minnie and Gnasher appeared in the next chamber.

It was a huge, empty, black dome-shaped space, lit only by the small lights in the floor.

"Welcome! To the game of tomorrow!" came a voice from nowhere.

Suddenly, a huge hologram of a Viking head appeared in the air above them.

Huge holograms and Viking heads are two things that don't belong together. It looked weird. A hologram of a scientist or an alien works, but Vikings work best in carvings or paintings. Obviously, no one had told this guy.

The hologram looked down at Gnasher, Dennis and Minnie, and squinted.

"What's the deal here?" Dennis asked. "What subject is this?"

"Science!" the Viking hologram announced.

Minnie wasn't impressed.

"Science?" she said. "You're a Viking. Vikings aren't sciencey. They're fighty."

The giant floating head was offended.

"Why can't Vikings be scientists?" the Viking boomed. "I'll have you know I was the chief astro-scientist in Jorvik!"

"Whatever. So what do we have to do here?" asked Minnie, eager to get on with things.

"You have to read those giant balls of burning gas, the stars," the giant head said.

As he said this, the room was lit up by a thousand tiny points of light.

Well... I say 'a thousand tiny points of light'

because it sounds better than 'eighty-eight tiny points of light'. 'The room was lit up by eighty-eight tiny points of light' just doesn't have the same impact.

"**Whoa!** What's happening? I'm floating!" said Dennis.

He said this because he was floating.

"Hold on. Let me try something," Dennis said, and squeezed out a fart.

He shot up into the air.

"There's a giant ball of gas!" Minnie said.

"The history books have it all wrong. People think we astro-scientists studied the night sky for signs and messages in the stars... They never realised we could defy gravity," the Viking head said.

Dennis slowly floated up to the domed ceiling. Closer and closer to the... stars? The points of light looked like stars! And next to them were numbers.

"Oh, right! I get it now," Dennis said. "I've got to visit each star in the right order. How do I do that?"

First Dennis tried to fly like a superhero, but quickly found that no amount of thinking of moving forwards would move him forwards. He then tried waving his arms and legs about, and that sort of worked. Refining his technique (of thrashing his arms and legs around wildly), he started to move forwards. He realised he was swimming through the air!

"You've got to learn how to swim," his parents had told him when he was little. At the time he

Puzzle time!

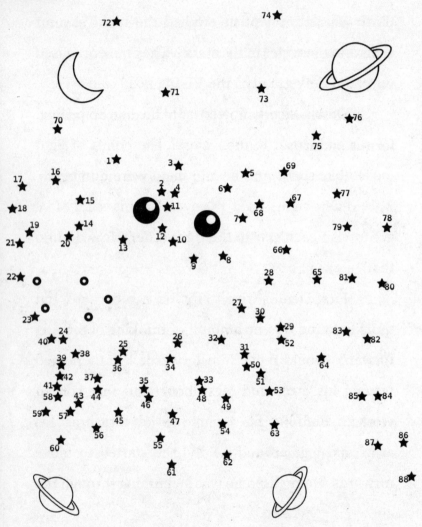

Join the dots to create a new constellation.

wasn't sure, but now he knew why. You never know when you're going to find yourself floating around a holographic model of the night sky, in a secret underground cave under a museum.

Slowly he began to join up the dots of light, to form a picture.

Eventually, arms and legs aching, Dennis floated back down to Earth.

Okay, that's not strictly true. What happened was he swam back down towards the ground then, moments before he reached it, the holographic Viking scientist turned gravity back on for him and he fell the last few centimetres.

The floating Viking head thought it was hilarious!

"Ha! Ha! Ha!" he laughed. "That's never not funny."

Dennis disagreed. "Are we done?" he asked.

"Ha! Ha! Ha! Yes!" the Viking said. "Unless you want to stay for holographic cakes and biscuits?"

IT'S ALL WEIRD

Meanwhile, Mayor Wilbur was sitting happily in his office high in Beanotown town hall. He spun round in his lovely big chair and looked out, down onto the streets of Beanotown. The quiet, boring streets of Beanotown.

In the distance, the custard factory didn't explode. No hot-air balloons full of eccentric millionaires fell out of the sky. The bank wasn't robbed. In the top-secret research station, no one dropped any canisters of strange gas, which didn't turn anyone into zombie clowns. Over in the park, no dinosaurs escaped Duck Island. No time travellers appeared at the police station warning of impending doom. Just outside the town hall, a tanker full of fizzy cola passed a truck full of those mints that turn cola bottles into fizzy fountains, and they didn't crash into each other.

Anything vaguely interesting you can think of

didn't happen. Think of something now that might have been mildly entertaining... thought of it?

That also didn't happen.

And it was all down to the lovely Golden Yawning Penguin of Boringness.

The Mayor looked at the Penguin and smiled. *I wonder how Walter's getting on?* he wondered, smiling to himself. *He probably has the Pea-shooter by now.*

Suddenly, everything around Mayor Wilbur started going all wibbly-wobbly.

"Arrrgh! What's happening?" he cried.

Quickly, he pressed the intercom button on his desk phone to talk to his assistant, Sandra.

"Sandra!" he cried into the phone. "Everything's going all wibbly-wobbly and there's some twinkly music. What's happening?"

From her desk just outside his office, Sandra (who was also Dennis's mum) spoke into the intercom.

"It sounds like a flashback, sir. Just go with it."

A few days before the start of this story, Mayor Wilbur, who had just got back from Yawntopia with the Golden Penguin, walked into Beanotown museum.

Having discovered that the Penguin in some way radiated boringness, he suspected there was something in Beanotown that radiated fun. It certainly would explain a few things. If there were such an object, it was probably in the museum, as the Penguin had been in Yawntopia.

He needed to find it and destroy it.

"You there!" he said to McGlinchy. "You run this place, do you?" he asked.

"Yes," said McGlinchy. "I'm the curator."

The Mayor looked at McGlinchy with suspicion. "Is there anything strange in this museum?" he asked.

McGlinchy looked round at the cyclops skeleton, the Viking steam-powered robot, Thor's

Toothpick of Justice, the six-horned triceratops skull, the Mitten of Doom, the time machine, the other time machine, the crystal skull, the iron skull, the custard skull, *The Book of Everything*, the Jade Cat of Indifference, the Little Yellow Elephant of Truth, the Spoon of Hope, the 6th century hamster armour, the Sholupog of Blergshmoo, the Shoe of Hope...

THE ONE-HIT WONDER

THOR'S TOOTHPICK

THE SHOLUPOG OF BLERGSHMOO

"It's all weird!" McGlinchy replied.

The Mayor raised an eyebrow. "Anything that might send out rays of fun or radiate weirdness?"

"Ah! Yes, actually. Cringebeard's Golden Pea-shooter of Everlasting Fun," said McGlinchy, who had no reason to think the Mayor wasn't a nice fellow. "The problem is," McGlinchy continued, "it's in the basement. Sort of basement. Things have got a bit out of control down there, if truth be told."

When McGlinchy told the Mayor what was going on in the chambers below, Wilbur thought it sounded dangerous. Anyone searching for the Pea-shooter might get hurt.

I'll send my son, instead! he thought.

* * *

Then the flashback ended and the Mayor found himself back in his office in the town hall.

Walter was a good boy. Soon, he'd have the Penguin and the Pea-shooter. The Mayor knew that he probably wouldn't be able to control the Pea-shooter.

No matter! he thought. *If I can't control it, I'll destroy it and make sure Beanotown stays this way forever. I win either way!* He liked that. The idea that he would win either way.

The Mayor strolled over to his new inanimate chum, the Penguin, and patted it on the head. It was quivering. Shaking. Vibrating.

"Pedro!" He'd named it Pedro somewhere along the way. "What's wrong with you, you stupid thing? Cheap overseas rubbish."

For the first time in a while, the Mayor thought *Uh-oh.*

KA-CHUNK! THUNK! BISH!

Dennis, Minnie and Gnasher were now in PE. Or at least the PE challenge. It was obvious. It had the floor. You know. That wooden floor with the coloured stripes. That floor. Only this floor was huge! The hall was misty and it was impossible to see from one side to the other.

KA-CHUNK!

Dennis and Minnie felt the floor shake and gave each other a puzzled look.

KA-CHUNK! came the sound again, out of the mist. KA-CHUNK! THUNK! BISH!

Dennis was hit in the face by a basketball.

When Dennis and Minnie told me this later, when I was interviewing them for this book, I couldn't help but smile. If you remember from the start, Dennis had accidentally managed to kick a ball into my own face several times. Dennis lied, actually,

when he told me his version and said the ball missed. I got the truth out of Minnie. She said, "Then **BOSH!** A basketball flew out of the mist and smacked Dennis right in the mush! You should have seen it! It was awesome! His face went all fat and red. As red as the stripes on his jumper. Classic!"

"It's dodge ball!" Dennis shouted. "We have to get across the court somehow."

KA-CHUNK! KA-CHUNK! A 9-foot-tall, rusty, steam-powered robot stepped out of the mist. Dennis and Minnie only spotted that it had a large hole in it's chest when – THUNK! – a basketball flew out of it.

KA-CHUNK! KA-CHUNK!

Another steam powered robot appeared.

"These are those steam-powered Viking robots," Dennis pointed out. "Remember? There's one up in the museum. In the olden days they probably shot cannonballs."

"Well, duh!" replied Minnie.

Dennis spotted a vaulting horse. You know, one of those things you jump over in PE.

KA-CHUNK!   KA-CHUNK! THUNK!

He ran over and took cover behind it. The others followed.

KA-CHUNK! GNASH! POP!

Gnasher had popped a ball with his teeth!

Dennis poked his head above the box. **THUNK! BISH!** A basketball smacked off his forehead.

"Arrrgh!" he shouted. "What did I do to deserve this?!"

"A lot of people just don't like you," Minnie helpfully pointed out.

"Okay, it looks like there's another box up ahead. If we keep going, I think we can make it to the double doors at the far end," Dennis told them. "Gnasher, can you cover us? Pop as many balls as you can."

Gnasher nodded, drooling with excitement.

"Ready?" said Dennis. "3, 2..."

But before he could finish, Minnie ran off into the mist.

"Catch me if you can, slowcoaches!" she called back.

Dennis gave chase, followed by Gnasher.

Dennis had almost caught up, when – SHOOF! – a hole opened up in the floor and Minnie fell down it. There was no time to stop. The only thing Dennis could do was jump over the hole. Landing on the other side, he slid behind the next box just as – THUNK! BOING! – a ball was fired at him and it bounced off the box.

Ever done that? An awesome cool move when there was no one around to see it?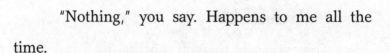

"Ha! Ha! Ha! Yes! **Did you see that?!**" you shout.

"See what?" they say, turning round.

"Nothing," you say. Happens to me all the time.

Dennis looked back at the hole in the floor, waiting for Minnie to climb out of it, but she didn't.
SHOOF!   SHOOF!   SHOOF!
Other holes were appearing in the floor all around both him and Gnasher.

Minnie fell and fell. She fell down a long pipe that at first went straight down. Then slowly changed angle until she was slithering down like a slide. Suddenly, the pipe bent and somehow she was going up. Ahead of her she saw a light.

A few seconds later - WHOOOSH! - she fell out of the pipe and landed in a heap.

"ARRRGH!" she screamed.

She was sitting on carpet.

Minnie looked up and saw a yeti. Unfortunately she was currently screaming, so had nothing else to do but change the tone of her scream a bit. **"ARRRGH!"**

"Shush," said the yeti, putting its finger to its lips, and pointed to a sign that read 'Quiet, please', before calmly walking off.

Minnie looked around. She was in the Beanotown library! She should have guessed, what with the yeti and all (the librarian in Beanotown is a

yeti. Don't ask. That'll take a whole other book. My publisher's already booked her holiday).

The library was, without doubt, the best building in Beanotown. It's all modern and glass and friendly and new (it was the last thing to be built before the Mayor took over and started pinching town money for himself). The whole buliding had even been designed and built in the shape of a book.

Minnie liked the library. It could be a source of lots of posh new words to bug Mum with. But this one time she thought, what with the fate of the town at stake, she should probably be elsewhere.

THUNK! GNASH! POP!

Looks like we're on our own," Dennis said to Gnasher, back under the museum. "It can't be that far now." He looked around for the next box. *How did Walter do this?* he thought.

KA-CHUNK! KA-CHUNK!

The robots were moving around to aim at them.

"They don't give you long to rest!" Dennis said to Gnasher, and made a dash into the mist.

SHOOF! Dennis heard the sound of a hole opening up. **SHOOF! SHOOF! SHOOF! SHOOF!** The sound was repeated again and again. Some loud, very near him. Others quieter, off in the distance. One opened right in front of him and Dennis jumped over it, but another hole opened up right where he was going to land!

He reached out and managed to catch the edge of the second hole. Gnasher jumped right over him.

KA-CHUNK! KA-CHUNK! KA-CHUNK! KA-CHUNK!

The robots were catching up. It was a good job they were slow, even if the basketballs they shot were fast. Dennis scrambled up out of the hole. **THUNK! BISH!** A basketball bounced off Dennis's back.

Gnasher's reactions were very fast. He spat out the bits of gnashed-up basketball and gave Dennis a *'don't you wish you were me?'* look.

Find your way through the maze. Start at the bottom and finish at the top. Careful of the robots!

Dennis squinted through the mist and saw the double doors loom up out of it. Next to the door he saw another vaulting box, with the top taken off.

"Urrrgh!" Dennis groaned. "Walter climbed inside a box and just pushed it along from the inside. He used it like a tank! He wouldn't have been touched."

Gnasher gave Dennis one of those *'I bet you wish you'd thought of that'* looks.

Up on street level, Minnie ran out of the library. She had to get back to the chamber to help Dennis.

Unfortunately, there was an ice cream van outside the library, so she forgot what she was supposed to be doing and got an ice cream instead.

THE WORLD'S MOST POWERFUL COMPUTER

Stencilled on the door in front of Dennis and Gnasher were the letters 'IT'.

"Sweet!" Dennis exclaimed. "I'm good at computers. This'll be awesome. It'll be all super crazy advanced. It'll be stuff out of an alien spaceship that crashed thousands of years ago, or something."

Then a look of realisation ran across his face.

"And I know the exact spaceship!" he said. "That spaceship that got trampled by a mammoth when I was stuck in that ice age. This is going to be amazing!"

Quickly, Dennis opened the door and was instantly, hugely, disappointed.

"What's all this junk!?" he shouted.

The kindest word you could use was 'retro'. This would have been high-tech in the 1950s, but now it was well past its sell-by date.

There was a large desk in the middle of the room. Set into it was a bunch of old small TVs surrounding a larger old TV and a bunch of dials.

The large screen in the middle lit up and a friendly cartoon face smiled at Dennis. "Hello!" it said. "I am the world's most powerful computer."

"No, you're not," Dennis told it.

"A computer is an artificial thinking machine. One day in the far future everyone will have a computer room in their house," it continued.

"I've got a computer in my pocket," Dennis told the machine, pulling his mum's rubbish old phone out of his pocket.

The computer seemed a bit angry. **"I am the world's most advanced machine."**

"What year do you think this is?" Dennis asked.

"1951," the computer answered.

Dennis rolled his eyes. "What do I need to do?"

"Use the logic gates to find the passwords," the computer told him.

"These dials are logic gates, yeah?" Dennis said, noticing the readout read **1010 1110 0100 0110**.

The first number was one. Dennis turned the centre dial to one. This meant the first word of the sentence was on the right. He followed the line to the next dial. The next number was zero, so he turned the dial to zero and followed the line to the next dial. The next number was one, which led to a final dial.

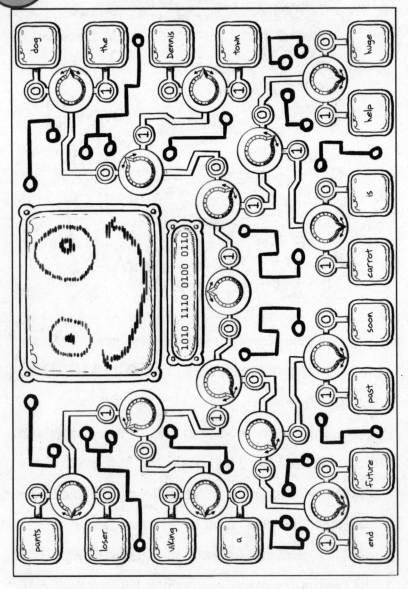

Can you crack the code by following the lines to the four words that make up the sentence?

The final number in the first set was zero, so Dennis clicked the dial up to zero and the nearest screen lit up. It said 'Dennis is a loser'.

Dennis was furious. "How is that the sentence? You think it's the fifties! How is that even the sentence?"

"There was a boy in here earlier. He may have done a little bit of reprogramming," the computer told him.

"Arrrgh!" Dennis screamed, **"Walter!"**

Suddenly, the room began to shake.

"Uh-oh!" said the computer. "That's not good! You'd better go through to the final challenge."

A HUGE TIDAL WAVE OF UNCONTROLLABLE NONSENSE

Dennis and Gnasher staggered into the last chamber, the ground beneath them shaking. The Golden Pea-shooter was in the centre of the room...

... in Walter's hand!

And Walter was on the back of what looked like a giant Gnasher. Only this one had a longer neck, its front legs were too short to reach the ground, and it's back legs and tail were much bigger. It looked like a Gnasher, but it was the same shape as a T. rex. It was a Gnashersaurus rex!

That thing must have come from Duck Island! Dennis thought, remembering what Gran had said after her flashback. *She wasn't wrong when she said it looked a bit like Gnasher.*

(See. I told you back near the start that the bit about dinosaurs surviving was going to have something to do with all this later, didn't I?)

Good books have lots of descriptions about things. I should describe the big cave they were in with stalagmites and other stuff, but really the only thing you need to know is that Walter had won!

Dennis had completed all the challenges in the Chamber of Mischief (sort of), but he'd got there second. Walter had won!

Walter had the Pea-shooter and, more awesomely, he had a dinosaur! Dennis had always wanted a dinosaur. And somehow the Pea-shooter gave Walter power over the Gnashersaurus rex. He was riding it as if it were a pony.

Grrraaa! roared the Gnashersaurus rex, but Gnasher wasn't afraid. Dennis was in danger, so Gnasher ran forwards and across the bridge, to protect his friend.

SWOOOSH!

The Gnashersaurus rex spun round and, with a flick of its tail, knocked Gnasher into the water.

Okay, maybe there's something in books properly describing places. Don't tell my old English teacher I messed up with this bit!

There was a circular platform in the middle of the room, with a narrow bridge leading to it. Under

the platform, beneath the bridge, ran a fast-flowing underground river. It was this river Gnasher had just fallen into. It would have been loads better if I'd mentioned that before. Apart from that, though, there's nothing else I should have mentioned.

"Gnasher! No!" shouted Dennis as he looked down into the rushing water.

Gnasher could not be seen.

"You lose!" shouted Walter. "You lose big time! Ha! Ha! Ha!"

He seemed different, somehow. More confident, maybe?

"I'm meant to take this Pea-shooter thing back to my dad so he can destroy it. But you know what? I'm keeping it! Ha! Ha! Ha! Come on, Genghis! Let's wreak havoc on the surface!" And with that, he took his new pet up the huge stone steps.

Okay! Okay! I should have said there were huge stone steps at the far side of the cavern.

Walter's changed, Dennis thought, remembering what McGlinchy had said earlier about the Pea-shooter affecting Gran, making her more reckless. The same was happening to Walter.

***

Nearby, in the town's top-secret research station (every town has one), Professor von Screwtop was putting the finishing touches to his latest creation, a service robot. I say 'finishing touches', but really it had been finished days ago. Von Screwtop just couldn't get the thing to work.

"Come on, you stupid thing!" he shouted at the tall round-bodied machine. "Work! There's cooking to do! Cleaning! Lifting! Carrying!"

The robot had been awake for days, but didn't like the idea of a life of all that work, so it just stood still and

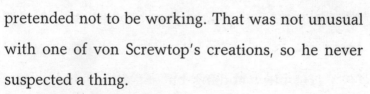

pretended not to be working. That was not unusual with one of von Screwtop's creations, so he never suspected a thing.

Out on the street, the bored people of Beanotown were starting to feel 'less bored'. Mainly owing to the annoying schoolboy on the strangely hairy dinosaur chasing them. In fact, less bored was putting it mildly. 'Terrified' would have been a better way of putting it.

"Ha! Ha! Ha!" laughed Walter.

Nothing had ever gone this well for him before. He'd won. He'd actually won! He was riding high on his own dinosaur!

Ahead of him, the townsfolk of Beanotown scattered. Walter held up the Golden Pea-shooter and asked himself, *How do you work this thing?* Little knowing that it was actually working already. Holding it gave him power over Genghis. It also gave him immunity to any weirdness going on around him. *Do I need golden peas for this thing?* he wondered, and put the Pea-shooter to his lips and blew.

He blew nothing but air at a fleeing estate agent. The estate agent's pants fell down and he followed suit. Walter raised an eyebrow. *Did I do that?* he wondered.

THEN THE PENGUIN EXPLODED

It's possible I may have given away what happens in this chapter with its title. If you don't like spoilers, you shouldn't have read the title. Because, as it says, in this chapter the Penguin explodes. Also, you shouldn't have read what I just wrote then, either. That'll spoil it, too.

Things in the Mayor's office were not as lovely as they'd been only a few moments ago. The general vibe had gone from 'no way to lose' to 'I'm going to lose everything!' in a really short time.

There was a commotion outside. The sound of screaming and what could only be described as 'dinosaury' sounds. Mayor Wilbur rightly assumed the two were connected. And Pedro was violently shaking.

The Mayor hugged the Penguin tightly, trying to stop the quaking idol from vibrating. Then it started to crack. Small ones at first then, quickly, large cracks.

"What's happening to you?" Wilbur asked of his boring buddy.

What was happening was Walter's fault.

Just as McGlinchy had thought, the Pea-shooter and the Penguin were in a sort of tug of war, only pushing not pulling, and using their powers instead of a rope (okay, so not really like a tug of war at all).

While the Pea-shooter was down in the Chamber of Mischief, there was enough distance between the two to stop anything happening, but Walter had brought them closer. He was only a street away. The tug of war that wasn't a tug of war was about to be won. Can you guess by which ancient magic item? No cheating. Don't read that bit earlier that tells you the Penguin explodes.

Suddenly, the Penguin exploded! It couldn't hold back the power of the Pranky monkey god any more.

BOOF! It tried its best to explode in the most boring way possible... and instantly turned into a cloud of gold dust.

The Mayor coughed.

"Pedro!"

He fell to his knees, threw up his arms and shouted to the sky in a scene so dramatic it wouldn't have been possible under the influence of the Penguin.

"NOOO!"... But yes. Pedro was no more. He was Pen-gone.

SOMETHING YOU DON'T SEE EVERY DAY

At an outlet water pipe near the lighthouse at Beanotown beach, a dog shot out onto the sand. It was the first time the pipe had spat a dog out. Gnasher shook most of the sand and water off, and looked out across the sea.

I'm at the seaside?! he thought as a giant octopus rose up out of the sea and grabbed the lighthouse with one of its huge tentacles. It pulled itself up onto the beach.

That's something you don't see every day! Gnasher thought to himself.

It felt totally natural to the giant octopus to come up onto the beach. It had been planning to, on and off, for 70 years or so. It had friended it's old school chum Addiron on Squidbook and had learnt that he'd got a job at the museum. The Pea-shooter hadn't made it do this. It was just a coincidence.

Across town, ace digger operator Julie J. Digson had hit a rock. She dug expertly round it. If this new road was going to be built, she knew this rock needed to go. As she dug round it, and the dirt fell away, it became clear how strangely smooth the huge boulder was. Julie tried to hook the boulder with the digger bucket.

The grey boulder moved easily. It didn't weigh anything like as much as it should do. Julie looked at the object. *Was that grey metal?* She bashed the thing with the bucket of the digger and with a clang, a perfect circle opened up. Julie got out of the digger

cabin to get a closer look. A closer look allowed her to see inside. It was a tiny alien spaceship. Unless you're a cat-sized alien, in which case it was a perfectly normal-sized alien spaceship.

Suddenly Julie heard, or rather felt, a piercing high-pitched whine. She clamped her hands over her ears, but it didn't seem to make any difference to the volume. Was she hearing it? Or was it in her head? Then it ended and Julie thought, *I hope that wasn't a signal to the alien's home planet!* Then she thought, *Why did I think that?*

But the Pea-shooter hadn't made Julie dig up the spaceship. It was just a coincidence.

Also, by coincidence, the Headless Headmaster of Horrible Hall decided that a walk in the park was just the thing.

And in the top-secret research station, Professor von Screwtop came back from the kitchen with his cup of coffee to find the robot he'd been working on gone.

Meanwhile, Walter was having a great time. He blew through the Pea-shooter at a retired policewoman and a bucket of water fell on her head. Even Walter was surprised at this. He looked up and saw that the office block he was passing was having its windows washed.

The window cleaner called down "Sorry!", but it wasn't his fault. He'd been distracted by the kid on a dinosaur going past. It was just a coincidence that he'd dropped the bucket when Walter had blown the Pea-shooter. Walter laughed. He laughed and laughed until the Gnashersaurus rex he was on ran into the giant octopus that was just outside the butcher's. Then he stopped laughing.

The Gnashersaurus rex was running round the corner and Gnashersaurus rexes don't have very good brakes, so it was unable to stop before ploughing into the squishy creature. The octopus didn't know this was an accident. It naturally thought it was being attacked, so fought back.

Walter flew through the air in much the same way you would if you rode your bike into a low wall and went over the handlebars. **SPLATCH!**

Walter landed in between the octopus's eyes.

The creature wrapped its tentacles round the Gnashersaurus rex and squeezed. That's how this particular giant octopus fought. By squeezing the life out of you.

GNASH! GNASH! GNASH!

The Gnashersaurus rex tried to bite the octopus but couldn't bend its neck enough. The octopus squeezed tighter.

***

Down the street and around the corner, Dennis climbed up out of the hole in the street made by Walter and the dinosaur.

***

Round the corner, the Gnashersaurus rex was finding it hard to breathe, it was being squeezed so much. Walter scrambled and slipped down the back of the giant octopus's head and was nearly to the floor when the Gnashersaurus rex began to roll beneath his feet...

Dennis dusted himself off, looked up and saw a Gnashersaurus rex wrapped up in a giant octopus rolling down the street towards him. On top of these two was Walter. Running.

Dennis dived back down the hole just in time. He looked up to see the strange combination bounce over the hole he was in. Dennis poked his head up just in time to see the Gnashersaurus rex, octopus and Walter crash into the town hall.

"That's something you don't see every day!" Dennis said to himself.

Then a large round-bodied robot walked past. It turned to Dennis and said, "Hey kid, if anyone asks, you ain't seen me, right!"

"Er, okay," said Dennis.

The robot passed a rather shaken-looking Walter lying on the pavement, picked him up and dusted him down.

"You look like you've had a bad day," it said, and walked off.

The Gnashersaurus rex untangled itself, got up, gave itself a shake and ran off.

The octopus shook its head and splotched off in the opposite direction.

"Which way's the park?" the Headless Headmaster of Horrible Hall asked Walter. "I'm quite lost."

"Arrrgh!" Walter and Dennis both screamed together as they ran off down the street.

"Things are spinning **out of control!**" Dennis shouted at Walter.

"Everything is **fine!**" Walter shouted back. "It's just one or two tiny coincidences. Nothing to worry about."

Then the aliens invaded...

WHAT IS GOING ON?!

You may be thinking at this point: *"What is going on?!"*

If you remember, earlier – much earlier, 70 years ago – Gran stuffed the Golden Penguin into the swimming cannon and shot it out to sea. But before everything went back to normal (for Beanotown), everything seemed to happen at once. A truck full of bouncy balls crashed into the railings on a bridge, and all the balls spilled out and bounced all over town! A dinosaur escaped from Duck Island (we've met him!). The main jam pipeline into town burst, flooding the precinct with strawberry jam. Lightning hit a candyfloss machine outside the amusements and created a candyfloss monster... and that wasn't the half of it.

This was, as you may have guessed, because the Penguin had held back the nonsense of the Pea-shooter. Like a dam. Allowing it to build up and up. When the Penguin left Beanotown, the floodgates were opened and the town had a mini nonsense flood.

It was going to be worse this time, however. All the nonsense and the fun and the bonkersness and silliness radiating from the Pea-shooter had built up over a longer period of time. There was loads of it now.

And the dam had burst!

A similar thing had happened to Yawntopia when the Mayor had taken the Penguin from there. Only because Yawntopia was already naturally boring (as opposed to Beanotown's natural loopy fun-ness), what happened was Yawntopia became a bit less boring but still quite boring. No one noticed.

SMUTCH BLOS THE SPLURGUNTZ

Finding out about Smutch Blos the Splurguntz was the hardest thing for me when I was writing this book. Everyone else was on Earth, but getting an interview with an alien that lives 'off-world' was tricky. There are hardly any buses that go there for a start. Anyway...

A lot of people think 22,000 years is a long time. That's because it is, unless you're a Splurguntz. Splurguntzs live for an incredibly long period of time. Put it this way... a six-million-year-old Splurguntz is still in nappies.

Twenty-two thousand years ago, Smutch Blos the Splurguntz was zipping past a little planet called Earth. It looked like a cold place, what with it being in an ice age and all, so Smutch Blos was going to leave it alone, but the ship's scanner picked up a strange signal. A crono pulse. Someone or something had just made a small hole in time down on the planet below. **A time traveller?**

Time travellers fascinated him and he'd only met a handful of them so far in his young 19-million-year-long life, so Smutch Blos decided to investigate.

Smutch switched to manual and swooped down through the atmosphere to where the pulse had come from. Visibility was poor owing to all the snow, but flying low he saw a human boy in a red-

and-black jumper, trying to run through the snow. Behind him was a huge woolly creature who, Smutch Blos assumed, must be the time traveller's pet.

Smutch landed and before he could get out, the time traveller's pet trampled his spaceship. **Wrecked it**, so it'd never fly again!

Smutch clambered out of his broken spaceship and eyed the time traveller. He was furious. There was no need to do that! He felt like saying something, but the red-and-black-jumpered time traveller was bigger than him, so he just pressed 'return' on his wrist device and teleported home.

Smutch Blos didn't know that the red-and-black-jumpered time traveller was there by accident, or that his name was Dennis.

Twenty-two thousand years later, Smutch Blos got a signal from his old ship. Someone must have dug it up. (Julie J. Digson.) He thought about leaving it, but he did like that ship; it was now a classic and maybe he could fix it up?

Twenty-two thousand years ago, Smutch had been a bit of a drifter. He hadn't done much in his first 19 million years of life. Except those 15,000 years in Art college. Since the mammoth trampled his spaceship, though, he'd pulled his socks up. He was now commander of the Splurguntz army.

So when Smutch showed up back on Earth, he showed up with that army.

A total of two hundred ships landed in and around Beanotown. The largest of which (which wasn't that large) landed in front of Dennis and Walter.

A door opened up in the side of the sleek craft and a ramp extended out, down to the ground. Out stepped Lord Smutch Blos, the commander of the Splurguntz army. The first face he saw was Dennis's.

"You!" he shouted, pointing an accusing finger at Dennis.

"Hey! I don't know what your problem is mate, but that thing with your spaceship wasn't my fault," Dennis quickly answered.

"You two know each other?" Walter asked unbelievingly. (Yes, 'unbelievingly' is a real word. I looked it up.)

"We met during the last ice age," Dennis said. "I don't want to go into it. Long story."

"You owe me a spaceship, buddy!" Smutch shouted.

"I owe you nothing! That mammoth was nothing to do with me," Dennis explained.

GNASH!

Gnasher leapt forwards.

"Arrrgh!" screamed Lord Smutch.

I should have mentioned before that as well as being cat-sized, Splurguntzs also look like cats, only green with two tails. And Gnasher is colour-blind.

Gnasher chased Lord Smutch Blos, the commander of the Splurguntz army, under a nearby parked van.

Dennis rolled his eyes.

"Okay, that dog is my pet, but there's no need to start an interstellar war over this."

"I'm starting an interstellar war over this!" came an angry voice from under the van.

GNASH!

came one of the biggest gnashes the world has ever heard as the Gnashersaurus rex gnashed down onto the van and picked it up with its teeth, revealing a very scared-looking Smutch Blos.

"Joke!" Smutch Blos cried. "I'm joking! No war!"

The Gnashersaurus rex spat the van out. It smashed into the street behind Walter and Dennis, and turned into a huge caterpillar for no reason.

"Whoa!" Gnasher exclaimed. "The weirdness is getting worse." Then Gnasher said, "Hold on! Since when can I talk? Red lorry, yellow lorry. The rain in Spain falls mainly on the plain. **I can talk!**"

"Weird stuff is starting to happen for no reason," said Dennis.

"There've been reasons for everything so far has there?" Walter asked.

"I don't know, maybe," Dennis answered.

***

Across town, Gran was lying in her hospital bed feeling very bored. Her hip clearly wasn't broken. She felt much better. Better but bored.

Then Gran's bed grew legs and ran out of the hospital.

SAID THE OSTRICH

"We can't evacuate the town in time," Dennis pointed out. "At any second, that shop over there could turn into a huge firework or something," he said, pointing at a phone shop, which promptly turned into a huge firework, complete with fizzing fuse.

"Don't give it ideas!" Walter shouted, flapping his arms about wildly.

"I said huge firework **or something!**" Dennis shouted as the fuse fizzed away, getting closer

and closer to the firework itself. "... Or something! Or something! Or something!"

The giant firework, complete with fizzing fuse, turned into an enormous wedding cake.

"Phew!" said everyone.

"Eventually, one of these random things will destroy everything," Gnasher said. "If, I dunno, Mount Beano becomes a volcano, that could be it for the town!"

In the background, Mount Beano turned into a volcano.

"Arrrgh! Everybody, don't say things!" Walter shouted.

"If we can't get away quickly enough, maybe we just need to get the Pea-shooter away from here," Dennis pointed out. He then grabbed the Pea-shooter from Walter, turned to Smutch Blos and said, "Dude! Take this and throw it into the sun."

"What? And turn the sun into a pair of huge underpants?" said Walter. "Don't be stupid!"

"OKAY Jupiter, or one of the other planets we don't use much," Dennis suggested. "Not Mars, though. I like Mars."

Suddenly, all across town, every Splurguntz spaceship turned into a doughnut.

"It did that on purpose!" Walter said, and then turned into an ostrich.

"Arrrgh! I'm an ostrich!" the ostrich screamed just as a clearly empty suit of armour ran past.

"Then we smash it!" Dennis said, throwing it to the ground.

DING! went the Golden Pea-shooter and bounced off the road without breaking. **"Don't do that!"** Gnasher shouted. "It might let everything out at once! That'd be instant destruction for the town."

"Typical Dennis!" said the ostrich.

228

A stone statue of a hippo wandered past. On its back was a model of a castle. The stone detention tortoise walked round the corner and their eyes met.

It was love at first sight.

"All this weirdness is coming out of this thing, yeah?" Dennis said, picking up the Pea-shooter again.

"Well, duh!" said a mushroom, which had up until recently been Gnasher.

Dennis held the Pea-shooter in his hand.

"What are you gonna do?" asked Gnasher, the mushroom.

Dennis put the Pea-shooter to his lips and... sucked.

Dennis's eyes turned white and glowed. He rose up into the air and turned into a fish, which turned into a cactus, which turned into an antique leather armchair, a desk lamp, a pie, an antique leather armchair covered with cactus spikes, a wardrobe... Dennis changed faster and faster until it was impossible to see what he was any more.

Around him though, things began to change back. The ostrich became Walter again. The giant caterpillar turned back into a smashed-up van. Everything returned to normal. Mount Beano was a mountain again. The doughnuts all became spaceships again and those spaceships all took off.

"Good luck with whatever this is!" said Smutch Blos, entering his ship before that, too, zipped away.

The only thing that didn't change back into the thing it was before was the stone hippo (who had been a motorbike until recently), the hippo who was in love with the detention tortoise. Some other power stopped that from happening.

The power of love.

Incidentally, in the tower on the hippos' back was a tiny prince. The tiny prince in the hippo tower and the tiny princess in the tortoise tower didn't fall in love. Actually, they didn't get on at all, but that's got nothing to do with the story.

Dennis changed and changed, into random, bizarre shapes that were never even things to begin with. Then, finally, he was a monkey. A Dennis-sized, glowing, green monkey.

The monkey laughed.

"Ha! Ha! Ha! I'm free!"

"We're in trouble now!" Gnasher gasped.

"Oh, now we're in trouble?!" Walter exclaimed. "Like before, with the aliens and volcanos, wasn't trouble?!"

The Pranky monkey god laughed. "I'm not really a god. Just an ancient being of immense power, taking the shape of a monkey," said the ancient being of immense power, made of pure energy, which was in the shape of... I'll just call it Pranky.

"Nice to meet you," said Gran, "I've heard a lot about you!"

"Dennis's Gran?" said Walter. "What are you doing here?"

"A few minutes ago, my hospital bed grew legs and ran out of the hospital. I thought to myself, *this is strange*. It turned back into a normal bed just round the corner," Gran explained. "Where's Dennis?"

"That sort of is Dennis," said Walter, pointing at Pranky.

"Let him go!" Gran shouted to Pranky angrily.

"Why?" asked Pranky in a booming voice.

"Because you'd like him," said Gran. "Can you access Dennis's memories?"

"Hold on," Pranky said, and squinted.

Dennis's memories flooded Pranky's mind. Countless tricks and pranks and assorted mayhem, most of the really good stuff seemed to be just by accident. Pranky laughed and down, out of the green monkey-shaped glow that was Pranky, Dennis fell.

"Ooft!" said Dennis as he hit the floor. "What happened? Was I a chair?! I remember being a chair at one point."

The ghostly shape of Pranky floated down to the ground and picked Dennis up.

"I've seen a few of your edited highlights," Pranky said. "You're alright in my book!"

He winked, then disappeared.

"Glad to have you back!" Gran exclaimed, giving Dennis a big hug.

"Katie?" came a voice.

Gran turned round. It was Leonardo McGlinchy.

"McGlinchy!" cried Gran, a big smile on her face. "I haven't seen you in years!"

"Hello, Katie," said McGlinchy. "The strangest thing just happened. One of the suits of armour at the museum came to life and ran out. I chased after it, but lost it a couple of streets away."

"McGlinchy loves you, Gran!" Dennis blurted out. "He's totes into you and I know you like him. So you know, whatever, but leave that till later. It always makes me feel a bit sick when old people snog."

"Shall we just start with a cup of tea and some biscuits?" suggested Gran.

"I'd love that," said McGlinchy.

"Earlier on, I escaped detention using *The Book of Everything...*" Dennis started to say to McGlinchy.

"Yes, that was me," said McGlinchy. "I was keeping an eye on your progress through the museum's CCTV and saw you were in trouble. I dropped it down into detention, because I didn't

want Walter to have the power of the Pea-shooter...
and also, you're Katie's grandson. I think maybe I've
been wrong all these years. You can't keep everyone
safe from everything."

"You just dropped it down?" Dennis said with
a look of disgust. "That thing nearly hit me!" Then
he smiled. "Anyway, it looks like the danger is past
now... and I got a cool new Pea-shooter!"

"I guess you can keep it," Gran said. "It doesn't
have that monkey thing in it any more."

Just then Minnie arrived, holding an ice
cream.

"Hey, whassup, guys?" she asked. "Have I
missed anything?"

THE END

OKAY, NOT QUITE THE END

Dennis was in a massive sulk.

"Why can't we just keep him?" he asked.

"Because he's a **dinosaur** and you already have a dog," said Dad. "He can go and live on Duck Island with the other dinosaurs. That's probably where he came from originally, anyway," Dad continued. "I'm pretty sure Duck Island's the only place with dinosaurs round here. Or anywhere."

"You just want to get rid of him because you saw the price of dinosaur food in the pet shop!" Dennis pointed out.

"Yes, I saw the price and it made me do one of my fast sleeps," Dad replied. "It was millions of years past its sell-by date, too."

"One of your fast sleeps? You fainted, you mean!" Dennis said.

"Whatever! We're not keeping it," said Dad. Then, turning to the Gnashersaurus rex, "Shoo! Go on! Go home!" And he pointed at the island in the middle of the duck pond. "I know it looks small, but it's big inside."

"You can't make him," Dennis said with confidence. "He totally loves..."

The Gnashersaurus rex stepped into the duck pond.

"... me," Dennis finished as the dinosaur waded out to, then into, the island without looking back once.

"Well, that's charming that is!" said Dennis.

Definitely

THE END...

Almost...

A FINAL WORD FROM THE AUTHOR

Phew! Well, there you have it. The totally true and not-at-all-made-up story of *Dennis and the Chamber of Mischief*.

I think, though, you may have guessed that there are more stories to tell.

As Dennis would put it, "There was that time that thing happened and that other time it kicked off, and that time when that other thing happened."

My publisher will want more detail than that, though. Ouch! I've just been pinged by a pea! *Who could that have been?* I wonder...

You owe me another story, Dennis...